R.I.P. ___?

Quidler and Peterkin came down the hall, looked in and saw Zott, came in cursing and got him down from the rafter.

"When the stiffs go nuts then the whole place is nuts," said Quidler. "How do you account for this?"

"How should I know? This whole business is unnatural so why should any particular part of it seem weird?"

Quidler cut Zott's belt with a knife and allowed the body to drop to the floor. "Maybe he isn't really dead!"

"You're always saying that! He's dead!"

"Sure, now that he's hanged himself. He's probably been up there for hours. I wonder why his pack didn't shut down."

Hauling Frye onto the floor, Quidler laid Zott on her bunk.

"Why did you do that?" said Peterkin. "Do you think maybe he feels bad and should be made a little comfortable?"

"I'm messed up, okay? I admit it. I can't bear the thought that one of these days they're going to send us a live one."

I lay on my bunk while something inside me screamed, "Me, me, me, me, me!"

Curt Selby
has also written
BLOOD COUNTY

I, ZOMBIE

Curt Selby

DAW Books, Inc.
Donald A. Wollheim, Publisher
1633 Broadway, New York, N.Y. 10019

FIRST PRINTING, SEPTEMBER 1982

1 2 3 4 5 6 7 8 9

DAW TRADEMARK REGISTERED
U.S. PAT. OFF. MARCA
REGISTRADA. HECHO EN U.S.A.

PRINTED IN U.S.A.

Chapter 1

I remember how the bottom of the lake looked as I was drowning. The thought of being buried in the mud frightened me more than the sensation of suffocating. My throat was jammed shut so that no water could go down but I wasn't thinking about air. I could feel my heart slow where at first it had thundered and leaped against my ribs as if it were trying to escape what was happening to it. It couldn't and neither could I. After a while I relaxed and drifted with the cold current while silence came to put me to sleep.

Funny how that nightmare was with me when I woke up in the cargo bound for Land's End. I apologized to Frye for being on top of the pile, not that I could help the way they stacked us in the crate, but she was in a snit and wouldn't respond to me.

Thoughts of death and life were in my mind, disturbing me, so I concentrated on the creaking and swaying cargo. My head felt strange, as if one piece of my brain were in a kind of trance while the other, smaller portion bellowed in terror and tried to attract attention. I didn't know which piece was me. Maybe both, maybe neither.

The packs were implanted in our brains on Earth so that all the driver had to do was think what he wanted us to do. Quidler got us moving as soon as the ship landed in the cradle. The compound was short of workers and had been waiting for the four of us for . . . I don't know, a long time, I guess.

Frye began squirming beneath me so I told her to take it easy and wait a minute until I rolled over and opened the lid. Inside of me the little piece of brain was doing a lot of yelling, as if it were scared and not sure of what was happening.

I shoved the lid too hard and broke the hinges. Frye came out behind me and I stuck out my hand and said, "Hi." I knew the difference between someone it was okay to talk to and someone it wasn't. Frye, LeMay and Zottinger were big dumb bunnies without much personality and not enough looks to make me feel self-conscious, so I felt right at ease with them, even when they ignored my greeting and didn't say anything back to me.

Land's End was a world of ice and snow, oases, aliens, factories, people who made me nervous and Peterkin.

"Move it, dum-dums!" said Quidler in a tone that said he was bored out of his mind. He gave me a particularly unfriendly stare as I walked down the ramp from the ship and I knew right away I wasn't going to get along with him. He was one of those insecure people who took an instant dislike to me because I was so big. About five-ten, he was contemptuous of tall women, especially tall and muscular women. Back on earth at the institution for hopeless cases, an acquaintance told me men liked muscles on women so I took up body building. I found out later she was no friend. Men didn't like muscled women, big women, or freak women. They liked cute little icebergs like Bates.

We were taken to the ground in an elevator, then for a couple of hours we stood on a motorized sled that slid over miles of gray ice until finally we arrived at the compound.

No sooner did we march into our quarters, which was a room fifteen by fifteen, than Zottinger climbed on a chair, slung his belt up over a ceiling beam, buckled it around his neck and did a jig in midair.

Frye selected one of the lower bunks while LeMay chose the other lower, at about the time I was sitting down on it. I threw her out so she climbed onto the bed above me. There were just bare springs and naked mattresses. Lying down, I looked up at the rusty metal and knew I could never endure such a view for very long. "Get out," I said. "I've changed my mind. I want that bunk you're on."

LeMay's head appeared over the side and she gave me a steady stare with her coaly eyes.

"No lip," I said. "I want us to be friends but I'll never take lip from anybody ever again. I have to have the top bunk."

We traded places and by and by the place settled down. The only noise was the creaking of Zott's belt as he hung swaying from the rafter.

"They want to freeze me to death," I said. "Are you cold?" LeMay didn't answer so I kicked the wall until she did. No, she wasn't cold.

Quidler and Peterkin came down the hall, looked in and saw Zott, came in cursing and got him down from the rafter.

"When the stiffs go nuts then the whole place is nuts," said Quidler. "How do you account for this?"

"How should I know? This whole business is unnatural so why should any particular part of it seem weird?"

Quidler cut Zott's belt with a knife and allowed the body to drop to the floor. "Maybe he isn't really dead."

"You're always saying that! He's dead!"

"Sure, now that he's hanged himself. He's probably been up there for hours. I wonder why his pack didn't shut down?"

"I suppose the belt wasn't that tight around his neck and he was getting some air."

Hauling Frye onto the floor, Quidler laid Zott on her bunk.

"Why did you do that?" said Peterkin. "Do you think maybe he feels bad and should be made a little comfortable?"

"I'm messed up, okay? I admit it. I can't bear the thought that one of these days they're going to send us a live one."

I lay on my bunk while something inside me screamed, "Me, me, me, me, me!"

"I want to know why he did such a thing," said Quidler. "You seem to be able to take everything in your stride. Maybe you can explain it to me. Why should he try to commit suicide?"

"It's the pack in his brain. Sometimes the stimuli hit the wrong chords or they liven up memory cells. One time I had one come up to me and ask me for a light."

"What if he's a maverick and keeps giving us trouble?"

"He'd better not," said Peterkin. "It's freezing in here. Let's get out."

The door shut behind them and again the place quieted down. Zott lay softly sniveling because his wife had run off; Frye brooded because her mother hated her; LeMay kept hanging her head over the side of the bunk to stare down at me with her sunken eyes. I think they made a mistake with her. She stank like a corpse.

Chapter 2

In my opinion, the work atmosphere was not conducive to optimum output. Too much heat, too much noise, no rest periods and no sense to what I did. Bates stood up there in the glass booth with the metal driver's hat on her head and drove us all day. It must have been boring but she was never sadistic or vindictive and was even considerate.

Do this, do that, went the urgings in my head and sometimes I obeyed, sometimes not. There was a big, open vat of molten metal in the middle of the room and looking at it scared me. "It's hot in here, isn't it?" I said to Zott. For a change he wasn't thinking about his wife, but he still didn't answer.

"You hot?" I said to LeMay. She was holding a smoking pipe in one gloved hand and flattened a knot on it with a steel hammer. Looking up at me with eyes sunken in black caves, she swung away at the pipe, missed and hit her hand.

"Ouch!" I said.

She didn't seem to think anything of it, kept whaling away at the pipe until it slipped from her crippled grasp and rolled away on the floor.

"You hot?" I said to Frye who operated a machine that fitted metal rings onto the edges of the ingots.

She wasn't hot. Do this, do that, said the unspoken signals in my head, running through my brain like my own thoughts but I could tell the difference. For a while I sat at my machine and made the rings Frye needed but then I got bored and tried walking toward the open vat. At about the time my eyeballs began to feel as if they were cooking, I backed off.

Plainly they didn't care about our feelings. The vat made the room too hot, about a hundred and thirty degrees in the corners, and I speculated as to how long it would take me to roast like a wedge of beef in an oven.

"You hot?" I said to Zott.

"Shut up. You make me sick with your whining and nagging. I work hard all day, I give you my pay and you spend it on your boyfriend."

I guess he had me mixed up with somebody else. "It's me," I said. "Don't you remember? I'm your roommate. Take a good look. You were never married to a woman like me. I'll bet I'm two feet taller than your wife and a couple of hundred pounds heavier."

He took a wicked looking rasp from a tool box and came at me as if he planned to stick it in me. Up in the booth, Bates yelled at him to go back to his machine. He liked me better, raised his weapon and lunged at me. I caught his wrist and held it while I tried reasoning with him.

"If there was some way I could provide you with a corpse I'd do it," I said to him. "If you could kill her maybe she'd be out of your system. That doesn't mean I'm going to let you poke me with that. Now knock it off!"

Later I wondered where he had come from. Where had they dug Zott up? Not literally, of course, since no one in Land's End had ever been buried. The very idea was incongruous. Still, it was interesting to think about. Maybe his bad temper had earned him a ticket to an execution chamber.

"You killed someone," I said to him after he calmed down. "Mind telling me who it was?"

Sitting at his machine with a sweet smile on his face, he looked up at me and appeared satisfied. "Your boyfriend."

Oh, well. Bates had a flunky come into the work area all decked out in an asbestos suit so that he wouldn't singe his precious hide. All that protection wasn't really necessary but the young ones seemed to prefer it. I think it made them feel more isolated from us workers. The first thing this one did was check the stitched hole in Zott's skull to make sure no wires were sticking out. Then he looked up at the booth and spread his hands to indicate that the world was indeed a bewildering place to be in. Bates pointed at me so he tried checking me out but I was too high up for him to reach my head.

"Sit down, dummy," he said.

I didn't feel like accommodating him and naturally I would never speak to him. He was one of those who were off limits to me. I knew the kind of person he was. He would make fun of me, spout insults, pinch my muscles to see if they were real, cast aspersions upon my identity.

"Sit down, dummy." Bates was telling me to do the same.

Frye forsook her machine and wandered over to see what was going on. At the same time Zott picked up his file and moved to stand beside me. He harbored no hostile thoughts but simply loved that tool. LeMay walked over and showed the flunky her hand. With his mouth open, he looked at it for a while and then seemed to realize for the first time that he was more or less surrounded by us.

"Yow," he said. No emotion or emphasis. Just, "Yow." He was too young for the job, in my opinion. Looking up at Bates in the booth, he said in a loud voice, "I don't care how much you offer me I'm not coming back in here! My job is in hydroponics!" He stepped away from the four of us and I guess the distance between us made him feel more secure. "Dummies," he said. "Brainless hulks."

"Get out of there if you can't control your emotions," Bates said over the intercom.

"Morons," the kid said to us. "How I loathe the sight of you. Why aren't you in the lousy ground where you belong?"

"Get out of there right now!"

"Somebody stinks real bad," he said. About then his voice broke or rose or did something emotional. Maybe he was feeling the heat inside his clothes. "No girls, no recreation, no entertainment, no human life," he said in a desperate tone. "Surrounded by a bunch of stiffs."

Bates was bellowing for him to get lost.

He opened his mouth and yelped like a dog abandoned in the middle of a prairie. "This place drives me nuts!" he said. "Who's dead? Sometimes I can't remember. Which of us? You or me?"

Chapter 3

LeMay's hand was a mess of broken bones, a flattened thumb and a tear in the flesh where a glistening shard showed through. Wondering if she would heal like a normal person, I pulled and hauled on her fingers until all the parts looked as if they were where they ought to be, after which I wound a rag around the whole thing.

"Leave it bandaged and it'll be better sometime."

"Where did you learn how to give first aid?" she said.

"I used to be a nurse. Well, not really a nurse, since I was too dumb for the work. Actually I was a nurse's aide."

"You're lying."

"Well, yeah, in fact I just hung around a doctor's office and saw how it was done."

Frye had a smoking hole in her back. After prying with a pin for a while, I dug out a buried hunk of metal that must have flown from one of the machines in the factory, or maybe a spark from the vat of molten metal caught her. Plainly nobody cared about us.

I couldn't tolerate the cold of our room after the intense heat of the factory so I went outside and down the hall and looked in all the closets. Finally I found some linen that wasn't for our use but for the flunkies quartered farther down the corridor. Who cared? Helping myself, I went back home and bullied my roomies into making their beds.

The temperature in the room was about forty, just enough to keep the walls from warping. What kind of treatment was that? I lay on my bunk staring at the

cracks in the ceiling and was grateful for the blankets. My
head felt funny, not like my old head but like something
weird. Somehow I felt more intelligent. My belly growled
and I thought about dinner .

"My mother never did like me," said Frye out of the
blue.

"Not that again," said Zott. He lay on the other top
bunk, not under the covers but upon them, like the
strange one he was. I wouldn't have called him an idiot
but he was odd.

Frye nodded as if her own voice and ideas were all that
existed in the world. "She had what you call change-of-
life skitz. For certain she wasn't playing with a full deck.
I'm never going to grow out of that period in my life. Not
ever. I'll never get rid of the scars."

"You know, that reminds me of my own past," said
LeMay. "I was just thinking—"

"I was talking. Why are you interrupting?"

"I was just thinking about the fuzz that shot me. He
only did it because I was black. They're all nigger haters,
all those pigs, even the black ones, but you'll never get
them to admit it. They get in the witness chair and talk
about carrying out their duty but it's all bull. There's
something wrong with fuzz, you know. I mean in their
heads."

"I was talking," said Frye.

"I remember like it was yesterday. That slug hit me in
the belly and the next thing I knew I was important.
Never in my whole life was I important until the minute
that goon plugged me."

"You've never been important," said Frye.

"Yes, I was. I lay on a white table and they said I was
worth more in simple dollars than anyone walking around
on the street because the pack worked. It doesn't work
with everybody. They put it in my head, not just any old
sawbones, either, but the best surgeons in the business.
They did it without ruining any surrounding tissue. I
heard them say so. Then when they were done, one of

them put on a driver's hat and told me to blink and spit and stuff like that."

Zott sat up in his bunk. "What kind of stupid directions are those? They had me walk around and do complicated things."

"I was talking!" said Frye.

I lay on my bunk wondering about the pack. I had one in my head, I knew, and I needed to know more about it.

"The idea," said LeMay, "is that a living person has a spirit that runs his motor. When the spirit is driven out by the body being killed or made unfit for habitation, then there's just the hunk of meat left to rot. The pack does the same job the spirit used to, not the same, of course, or not as good, but if you have a carcass and a pack and a driver then you have an individual capable of performing certain tasks."

"What can't they do?" said Zott.

"Usually they hardly ever talk, for one thing. The driver is in charge and—"

"Not of me, he isn't," said Frye. "To heck with Bates. She's a cute little iceberg but I'm a free thinker."

"Do you mind?" said LeMay. "Please don't interrupt. For another thing, workers can't do anything on their own. The driver tells them when to eat, when to go to the ladies' room—"

"How about the men's room?" said Zott.

"That too, except there's only one can up here for everybody. I know because I've tried it out a couple of times."

"They don't care about our feelings," I said. "What I want to know, though, is about the carcass and how it works."

LeMay settled back and continued edifying me. "The pack is a computer and a chemical kit that keeps the flesh alive. The blood is alive, the organs are alive, the carcass eats, works and eliminates, it doesn't stink or rot and it is super strong. All you have to do is stimulate the same old nerves with radiant energy and electrical impulses, and if you can stimulate the brain in the correct manner then the person will go on doing his job."

I didn't have to ask her about night time. I'd already had some samples of that. They couldn't completely shut the packs down at anytime or the body would begin to decay, so while Bates, Quidler, Peterkin and the others like them slept a normal sleep, the rest of us lay staring into space. There we remained until someone put on a driver's hat or used one of the little mechanical boxes most of the staff carried in their pockets.

Or no, we didn't remain there. I didn't. I wasn't like LeMay, Frye and Zott. I was different. Why or exactly how I couldn't say.

I had to admit those doctors were pretty good, but they must have made a mistake about LeMay. "Why don't you try some perfume?" I said to her, but she was staring into space and didn't answer me.

Chapter 4

Dinner was at six. Morning or evening, I couldn't say until I had been there long enough to tell the difference and know when the sun went down. All I knew then was that we ate at six o'clock after work. They didn't care how we felt. No napkins, paper plates, no salt or pepper shakers on the tables. To heck with LeMay, I ate half of her ration and she didn't complain. Maybe if she didn't eat so much it might improve her smell.

One of the cooks was a sow named Mildred who had something wrong with her normal, natural, spirit-stuffed head.

"What a moose!" she said, when I stopped in front of

her with my tray held out. Her buddies laughed and fortified her determination to make me look small, which
wasn't easy to do.

Maybe it was her poor appearance that caused her to
be so insulting. Certainly she didn't even look as good as
some of the folks standing on my side of the counter, except for her coloring. There she had the advantage. She
and her pals were prettily brown or tan or pink while my
companions tended toward sallow complexions, unkempt
hair and hollow looking eyes. Too, Mildred and her ilk
wore attractive clothes while we workers were dressed in
rags.

Never in this world did I ever or would I ever speak to
someone like Mildred. Not hangdog or anything like it, I
stood there waiting for her to put her lousy food on my
tray.

"There!" she yelped and put about three pounds of
mashed potatoes in the middle of my tray. They were
supposed to go in one little dent. "There!" she said, and
laid a foot-long steak on top of the spuds. Laughing fit to
kill, she put everything in one big pile and then stood
there giving me a gleeful leer. Since the tray was made
out of heavy paper, I didn't know if it was going to hold
up.

Mildred had tight red curls and a spotted nose. Her
teeth were big and white, probably false. Her bosom hung
out so far she probably hadn't seen her ribs in years. Oh,
well, she was a human being. Giving her an amiable wink,
I moved on down the line toward the dessert. Behind me
I heard a gasp followed by a thud and then the floor
shook as Mildred fell flat in a swoon. I didn't turn back.
The cake looked good, likewise the Jell-o, pudding and so
forth. The only reason why they gave us such attractive
food was that it was easier for the cooks to prepare for
the bosses and the workers at the same time.

Do this, do that, eating must have been a pain for the
other workers. As for me, I did what I pleased, cleaned
my tray and some of LeMay's. Up in the cafeteria booth,

Bates wore the driver's hat and talked to Quidler who sat beside her trying to make points.

Do this, do that, fork the junk into the hatch while keeping the glottis closed, then let it be swallowed into the gullet. Fork one, sip two, chew three, do it nice and don't make a mess. If you dropped your dinner on the floor, you mustn't step in it, and meanwhile Mildred was on her feet again and yelling that she wasn't going to stay on some backwater planet cooking for a bunch of stiffs who did things like real people and scared a person half to death.

It didn't seem right, me doing things the way I wanted while my friends had to have Bates call their shots.

"It's okay," said LeMay, putting a hand on my arm and leaning too close to me. Maybe some of that perfume I saw on the counter by Mildred's duty post? "I know you're worrying about us," said LeMay, staring into my eyes. I was surprised to see how green hers were. What with the dark circles around them, I had supposed they were brown. "You do your thing, we do ours," she said. "Okay?"

"But why am I different?" I said.

"I don't know. You've been fishing in our memory cells, fashioning personalities for us, making us talk, making us seem like something we aren't, trying to get answers to your questions. We don't have them. You'll have to try somebody else. Maybe Bates or Peterkin. You like him, I know. Maybe even Mildred could tell you some things."

"I can't talk to them. I have a complex."

"Then you'll just have to figure it out for yourself. We don't have the answers."

"I think you do. There's a lifetime of memory cells in your head."

"You can't wake all of them up, but if you could you shouldn't."

"Why not?"

"You might not like what you found."

I didn't care. All I had was time and days and occasions during which I could ponder, wonder and speculate.

"Bates is going to notice we're talking if you don't leave me alone," said LeMay.

"So?"

"It might be worse for you if they find out what you are. Have you considered that?"

I hadn't, for a fact. Was it possible that I could be worse off if Bates discovered I wasn't like the others? Possibly. I hadn't been worth a dime on Earth. Another fact: they didn't care about our feelings up here.

After dinner, after we had all done our stint of hit and miss with our meal, we were paraded down a corridor to the johns. Boys or girls, it didn't matter, even if we were modest, and we were made to go in and do this and that. They made us wash, too, so our skin wouldn't corrode from dirt and debris.

What did any of it matter? Oh, well, if I were to be considered just another carcass, I might as well make the best of it. Zott and I sat side by side and discussed the weather.

Chapter 5

A group of galley flunkies got bombed over the weekend and couldn't report for work detail Monday afternoon so Peterkin cut a squad from the work line and marched us out of the factory. It was okay with me. I didn't know where we were headed but at least we were getting away from the open vat and its blistering heat.

The back of the galley was a big long room painted battleship gray. Since we workers weren't supposed to have any spirits, there had been no effort made to lift us up with cheerful colors. We weren't normally in this area anyhow, since it was so important, at least to Peterkin who for some reason was bughouse about garbage disposal.

We had left Bates' area and were beyond her control and now Peterkin drove us with another smaller hat. His mental commands made my head feel different from the way Bates made it feel, tinnier or harsher or not so relaxed, or something, not that I cared that much. I could tune him in or out whenever I pleased.

The idea was for us to haul tubs of garbage outside to a big incinerator, which sounded like a simple enough task, but each tub was so bulky and heavy that it required two sets of hands. Peterkin wasn't at all proficient with the hat so that while two workers were carrying one tub through the door, everyone else fell down. He couldn't handle us all at once, couldn't slide from one head to another quickly enough. He got mad and started yelling so that everybody hurried around and did dumb things. Except for me. I was too busy staring at the frog sitting cross-legged on the floor by the exit.

He wasn't really a frog, naturally, but that was what people called him and his kind. He appeared to be just as interested in me as I was in him, left off casting longing glances at the overflowing tubs and gave me a long and careful scrutiny. He had picked me out of the line of workers right away, spotted me in an instant as if I were unique or different. Of course I wasn't, except that I was bigger than everyone and maybe that was what drew his attention to me. What else could it be? I was clean, I wore gray pants and a shirt, just enough to cover my nakedness and sure enough not sufficient to protect me from the air coming in the cracks around the door and windows. It was strictly northern.

The frog gave me a little smile and went back to drooling over the sight of our garbage. He wore only a pair of jock shorts, cast-offs from some human or worker. He nearly matched the drab color of the floor and walls which was why I hadn't noticed him right away. There was a spiny ridge running up his back and across the top of his head. The same ridge was on his upper arms and the front of his legs. Maybe his people had been aquatic at one time. I didn't know. He had human looking eyes but very small ears, a button nose and a little mouth. He sat minding his business beside the door while Peterkin displayed some of the worst of human qualities.

Finally I got tired of waiting for Zott to lift his end of a tub, raised it on my own and carried it outside.

"It's about time!" Peterkin yelled, to himself I think. He believed he was finally getting through to us. He wasn't, but the workers scarcely ever behaved in any predictable manner so he didn't know the difference. It was because he never really looked at us. No one did. A member of the staff gazing directly at my face or into my eyes was a rare experience for me. Except where Bates was concerned. She wasn't afraid to look at anything or anyone.

"Get those cans the devil out the door!" Peterkin yelled. "You, there, frog, get the devil out of the way. Can't you see you're blocking the lane?"

The frog was leaving anyhow, hot on my trail as I went out and stepped into a foot of crunchy snow. At least I had boots on. He was barefoot and hopped toward the incinerator as if he were supersensitive to cool temperatures. I discovered later that he was. Frogs were unfortunate in more ways than one. Their world was in the grip of an ice age and they had to live on the oases that weren't all that numerous. Their natural state, like everyone's, was nakedness, except that in their case it was most literal since they couldn't tolerate clothes touching their skin. As I tramped toward the incinerator with the tub balanced on my shoulder, I noticed the raw patches on this frog's back where the band of his shorts touched.

Behind me a pair of workers lugged another container. There were several frogs near the incinerator, all bone-skinny and shivering as if they were about to catch their death. At first I thought the attraction was the heat from the fire, and there was that, but the main lure was the stuff I was about to dump into the smoking maw.

"Here, you folks just take this stuff and you can have it," I said to the frog who had followed me.

They probably didn't understand my words but they read my actions well enough and were about to relieve me of the can when Peterkin came outside and did some more of his act. "You frogs get the devil away from my worker and quit pestering her about that trash! It won't do you any good asking her for handouts. She hasn't got the sense God gave a goose and can't do a thing on her own!"

Frog kept his eye on me but a downcast look began growing on his face.

"Baloney," I said. He didn't seem surprised, just became interested again and waited to see what I was going to do. Instead of dumping the stuff in the maw as Peterkin was directing me to do, I upended it onto the snow where the frogs could all jump at it.

"Workers aren't worth the powder to blow them up," Peterkin said when we were all back inside.

"Tell it to the vips," said a flunky who was supposed to be helping out.

"I want every bit of this garbage burned. That's the order and I want it done."

"There's only one thing wrong with that order. The vips never come here to see our garbage."

"Everything left over is to be thrown out," said Peterkin.

"That makes sense, like everything else in this environment. Most of the stuff left over from the tables is edible and a lot of it is just plain good."

"I hate this hat! I also hate those frogs! They give me the creeps!"

"Why don't you give that big moose fifty lashes for being disobedient? She's the one started everything." The flunky went away and left Peterkin talking to himself about wise guys and insubordination.

The flunky had been right about one thing. The garbage mostly wasn't garbage and I didn't mind that day's work at all. Every time I felt like it I snacked, and no matter how many times Peterkin came outside and hollered I upended a few cans so that the frogs could eat too.

Finally he had us line up—there were about twenty of us—and then he marched us to a deep snowbank and made us stand in it. "You're blamed well going to follow my orders or I'll keep you here until your feet freeze off," he said.

I wasn't worried about my feet, only the rest of me.

Do this, do that. "Feel it?" he said. "Feel my commands? You blamed well are going to feel them. I don't want any frog feeding! They're big enough pests without your catering to them. Let them go eat their own stuff and if they don't have any that's too bad."

Do this, do that. "You'd better listen to me," he said. "No dumping of tubs anywhere except in that incinerator maw!"

He had a fit when we started dumping the cans and all into the incinerator. The frogs kept running back and forth from the piles of food on the ground to a green oasis a quarter of a mile away. There were two bloody ruts from one point to the other. They filled empty gourds, big leaves, pieces of clothing, shoes, and then ran like crazy back home where they unloaded and came back for more. I saw a couple of them wearing boots but they bled worse than those who went barefoot.

"I hate this place," said Peterkin. He had us standing in deep snow again. Do this, do that. "Don't tell me that little iceberg named Shirley Bates can drive better than I. It isn't so!" Do this, do that. "No dumping food on the ground. I mean garbage. No dumping tubs in the maw. Just the garbage. There's a computer inside every one of your empty heads and I know you're capable of following simple orders. I'll leave you out here until your guts freeze solid if you don't shape up. All right, let's try it again!"

Bed never felt so good to me as it did that night. Shivering under half a dozen blankets, a big meal in my belly, I lay looking at the wall and wondered why Peterkin behaved as he did. I guessed he was upset.

"That's the wrong word," said Zott. "What he is is a contrary maniac. Frogs, workers, people, feelings, they're all the same to him: external and outside. What does he care?"

"You sound more like you're talking about Quidler," I said.

"No way. Quidler is rough but he has a soul."

"They all do. Only we don't."

"You know what I mean. Quidler has feelings."

"I think you're wrong," I said.

"You're looking at Peterkin's pretty face," said LeMay. "He's one of the swellest looking dudes I've ever seen, but that doesn't mean too much. I think Zott is right. Peterkin has a screw loose."

"Like my mother," said Frye. "She never had a full deck to play with. I remember when I was little I had to hide under the bed at night while she roamed around the house with a knife hunting for me."

Chapter 6

Bates came around to our room to conscript Frye and me for a special detail. It was okay with me since the factory and the galley weren't the best duty spots in the world. Or so I thought. After I got an inkling of what was going on in Bates' mind I thought better of my ordinary jobs. She didn't take Zott along with us because she didn't trust him.

"I think he's got some wires crossed," she said, leaning over the bunk and staring into his eyes. "One of these days I'll have his head opened to see if the pack is causing pressure or something." Straightening up, she looked around and sighed. "There I go talking out loud again as if I had company." To me she said, "Who am I talking to? You?"

I almost nodded. It was difficult not to like her or sympathize with her, or something. She always looked as if someone was about to push her off a plank, as if she were on her last leg, as if fate continually dealt her a losing hand. Short by my standards, she had cropped yellow hair, big clear blue eyes and a trim body. Usually she wore a little smile on her face, as if she would never cease marveling over all the mysteries she encountered.

Today she wore a driver's hat but it wasn't the big one she used in the factory booth but was more like a tam that fit behind her ears.

"Come along, you two," she said. "Mutt and Jeff. Let's go fight with nature."

I didn't mind being called Mutt. I used to read the funnies, or at least I looked at the pictures.

Before we went outside she provided us with jackets and hats. "No matter what they say, you aren't going out without these," she said. "If anybody makes a crack about it I'll dock them a week's pay."

I didn't know if Frye cared but I appreciated my jacket and was glad to have it. A motorized sled took us in a terrible hurry across ice and snow, about thirty miles, to a steeple of steel that went up so high the top was hidden in clouds.

Oil was pumped up through a pipe into lower levels of the steeple where big bags sucked it in and were hauled by cable to the top spires, which were a few thousand miles above the planet. There the anchored bags floated in weightlessness until tugs towed them to the pipeline.

One glance at the door of the steeple elevator waiting to gobble us up was all I needed to make me want to back away but there was the choice I had made about maintaining my pretense, so I went ahead and stepped in.

My stomach dropped like a quiet bomb all the way to the top.

Bates was annoyed when she saw who was waiting by the entrance to the ship. "Where's Quidler?" she said.

Peterkin gave her a friendly smile. "Tied up. Couldn't make it. I hope you don't mind."

"I do mind but I'm in too much of a hurry to go back down now. Get inside and into your suit."

Do this, do that. Frye and I were sent to our seats beside a box of buttons and lights. It wasn't much of a ship, didn't look anything like a Flash Gordon or a Buck Rogers job but was just a long cylinder with banked panels and a pair of raised platforms for the pilots.

"You dum-dums had better do your jobs right," Peterkin said as he strapped himself into the co-pilot's seat.

"They do as they're told, which is more than you do," said Bates. She put on her suit, strapped in and sent the ship climbing up the tracks toward the sky.

Peterkin sat idly and didn't do much more than watch. "The trouble with you is you don't know how to relax."

Bates didn't respond, simply flew the craft up out of the maw and headed for the nearest floating bag of oil.

The pipeline was anchored between the five planets in the solar system, a massive structure that was kept in position by on-board jets and computers. The idea was for the people in Land's End to take the oil out of the ground, transport it up here and put it in the pipe so that the other planets could send their own barges and draw on the fuel whenever they pleased.

The oil bag was moored to the steeple by a long line. Bates maneuvered around the tether in order to connect the rear end of the ship to a dangling hook some quarter-mile from the bag. From there we slowly tugged the burden off into the black sky toward the pipe that was like a huge and uneven ring floating in the middle of nothing. Off to my left I could see Land's End but I really had to do some gawking to spot another of the planets.

Positioning the ship near to the pipe, Bates made ready to go outside, with Peterkin right behind her. Before he went through the door he turned to give Frye and me a grim stare.

"What's the matter, afraid they're going to get even with you for tormenting them?" said Bates.

That made him angry. "If I was afraid of anything about them I'd shove them through the airlock!"

"The devil you would. They're company property and I'm liable for them."

"Creating them in the first place was a mistake. In fact it was a crime against nature."

"I agree," said Bates. "They belong in the ground."

"I don't mean it that way. Just because they're cheaper than machines isn't a good enough reason for their existence. It goes against my grain to work with them."

Outside, the two of them swam through the black while Frye and I watched them through a port window.

"She doesn't like him," said Frye. "I don't blame her."

"That's ridiculous," I said. "He's a fine-looking person."

"So was Genghis Khan."

"Knock it off and do your job."

"I forget what it is."

"Watch those green buttons on that box. If they change color, push that brown button."

"That doesn't make any sense. Why do they make things so complicated?"

With a shrug, I said, "I don't know. That's the way their minds work. They have a lot of brains."

"Not like us, huh?"

Outside, Peterkin grabbed hold of Bates' foot and hauled her toward him. They both floated off course until she slammed him in the side of the helmet with a wrench and he let go.

She opened a valve on the pipe and wound a loose cord from the oil bag around it. Automatically the valve began winding up the cord so that the oil bag was drawn nearer. Peterkin swam to the rear of the tug to disconnect the bag. As soon as the fat container was tight against the pipe, the buttons on Frye's panel blinked blue.

"Push the button," I said. So did the packs in our heads as Bates began talking to us from her position outside. I was the backup, in the event that my companion failed to perform.

"I forgot which one," she said.

"The brown one."

"I don't feel like punching it."

"They didn't bring us all this way to have you say that. Push the brown button."

"It's so dull-looking. I feel like pushing the yellow one." She did.

Outside, the valve on the pipe disconnected with the bag instead of sealing tight and the oil started coming out. Bates and Peterkin swam away and headed toward the craft's airlock as quickly as they could.

It was all automatic, like an elevator. Once you gave a signal, the thing was done with no way to change it. Overriding a signal was a good idea but it meant more expensive computers that were seldom used in tug operations. I punched Frye's brown button so that the yellow one went off but it didn't make any difference about the oil still coming out of the bag, about a million gallons of it, and if the company was lucky the stuff wouldn't wrap itself around the pipe and cover up some important mechanisms. This time they were lucky. The rapidly congealing blob lay to starboard of the pipe, all spread out like a crystalline web that occupied a large portion of space.

Peterkin came in cussing at the top of his lungs, with Bates right behind him.

"See, what did I tell you? The panels are the right color now," he said. "These two clowns changed it!"

"Don't be asinine. Whatever happened had nothing to do with them. Get in your seat so I can back out of here and get a snare around that mass."

"I resent being called asinine! A million gallons of oil! They'll have your neck for this! They'll have my neck!"

"That's okay with me. I'll accept a desk job anytime they feel like transferring me."

Peterkin strapped himself into his seat. "I still say it was them. Those dummies!"

"I must have gotten my orders crossed," said Bates, her tone puzzled.

"Don't tell me you're less than perfect!"

Bates cruised to what she thought was an appropriate position and then they left Frye and me alone in the ship again while they went back outside to string a snare around the oil blob. There were two kinds of snares, one with holes for hauling solid objects that required exposure and one without holes for hauling liquids. Through the pack Bates told me which button to push. For the longest time I hesitated so that she had to repeat the instructions. I wanted to obey but besides feeling sulky because of all the insults that had been sent my way, I was full of curiosity. I pushed the wrong button so that the holey snare was jettisoned.

Bates and Peterkin didn't know the difference since both huge coverings looked impermeable. It took them several hours to get the thing around the frozen blob of oil and by the time they came back inside they were exhausted.

The idea Bates seemed to have in mind was to take the sack of oil down through the atmosphere into the sky of Land's End, target it over a shallow crevasse or culvert in an abandoned area and let it drop. That way it could be salvaged without too much trouble.

First she filled the inner lining of the snare with ice, several yards of it, after which she increased the weight of the ship by using the gravity engines. By the time the craft neared the planet's atmosphere it was so heavy it plummeted like a rock.

It would have worked if I had punched the right button. As we entered the sky of Land's End, the ice in the snare had melted and the pile was smoking. While Bates was slowing down, lightening the gravity of the tug and thinking about looking for a volcano or other crater in which to dump the oil, the snare began to leak.

Some one hundred miles from our factory compound, a

colony from Earth had built a transparent dome and was doing some experimental living inside it. At about the time everyone was sitting down to dinner a million gallons of oil hit the roof.

No one was killed but the experiment was ended and the dome's inhabitants had to be rescued by rafts.

Chapter 7

So many quiet days went by that I began to think Frye and I were going to get away with what we had done. Not that my friend had much of a hand in what happened.

As usual I was wrong. One evening after dinner as I lay under a pile of blankets trying to keep warm, Peterkin came into the room with a driver's hat on his head. First he had to see what he was doing, otherwise he might activate Zott and LeMay, which he didn't want to do.

The only reason there was a light in the room in the first place was for the staff. It certainly wasn't for us. At any rate Peterkin switched on the overhead light and immediately became upset because our beds were made. No doubt he anticipated seeing a bunch of stiffs decorating bare mattresses. It reminded me that Bates had seen the same thing but hadn't been bothered by it. I guess she must not have noticed or maybe she thought Quidler did it. Not so Peterkin.

He made little whining sounds in his throat and backed toward the open door as if he intended to go out but he hit the edge and made it slam shut.

"Madness!" he said, feeling behind him for the knob. In a louder voice he said, "Insanity!" Yanking open the door and rushing out into the hall, he yelled, "Who did it?

Who's the wise guy? Who gave linen to the dum-dums? Every one of you flunkies is going on report! Either we get a change of personnel around here or I intend carrying my complaint straight to the top man!"

He stomped away and didn't come back until just before dark. Meantime I had gotten up and turned off the light because it bothered me when I was trying to sleep. Right away I knew when he came back in, not that he was using the driver's hat for he was too busy muttering over the fact that the light should still be on. Nobody ever came into these quarters, so who turned it off? Evidently he satisfied himself, because he lost his fear.

"Good evening, girls," he said, standing beside my bunk and grinning. He wasn't upset or whining anymore but seemed calm, amiable and full of intent.

While he drove us away from the compound and into the icy wilderness on a sled he told us all about it. Frye and I had gotten him into a lot of trouble with the company. Not Bates, oh, no, never frigid little Shirley who could do no wrong. Of all the companies drilling for raw materials on all the populated planets, she was the manager with the best record. Did Ms. Bates have a problem during a mission to the pipeline? It couldn't possibly be her fault so who had gone along with her? Two dumdums and a live one, eh? Then the live one was to blame for the trouble, of course and naturally. Tie his rear in a sling and roast him over the coals for a while, and dock his pay at the same time! Never mind that Bates had tried to put in a good word for him. It was just for show.

Frye and I stood on the sled while Peterkin sat behind us operating the controls. He wore a heavy parka and hat while my friend and I had on only boots, pants and shirts. I nearly froze during that journey while the driver griped and yelled at the brisk wind whipping through a prairie of ice dunes.

He refused to believe that the domed colony had been wiped out by accident. The target might have been coincidental, but from the beginning of our mission to the pipeline everything had gone wrong. Since Bates hadn't been to blame and since he surely hadn't done anything out of line, that left the girls. The dum-dums. The big stupid-looking one and the brown one. Naughty, naughty.

The gales whipping between those big dunes nearly turned my hair white. Overhead, the sky was gray and filled with swirling clouds. In a little while night would come. An angry but triumphant Peterkin drove the sled a long way from home and made us get out. At the last minute I think he forgot we weren't real people.

"You two walk over there by that big dune and wait for me to come back for you," he said.

Did he really believe we had deliberately crossed him in the tug and did he actually think we could do something like that on our own? I don't know. At the time I couldn't be sure about that or anything else, except for one item: he was lying when he said he would return for Frye and me.

As soon as he drove the sled far enough away for the influence of the hat to wane, Frye fell down on her back to collect wind in her mouth.

"No, you don't, you're not pulling that mindless stuff on me," I said. "Not now when I sure don't want to be alone. Get up!"

Crawling to her hands and knees, she looked up at me and then stood. We stayed by the dune with our arms around one another while I tried to figure out if there was the remotest chance that Peterkin might come back for us. I sincerely doubted it. Plainly he was so mad at us that he had decided to murder us as if we were living, breathing women. The only thing wrong with that was that one of us was.

I could get no satisfaction from hugging my companion who was only slightly less chilly than any of the dunes surrounding us. For some reason I began thinking about the lake back on Earth. It had been cold there, too, perhaps not this cold in the beginning, but eventually it felt every bit as uncomfortable.

"I don't want to think about it," I said through my

chattering teeth. "I can't stand it when I remember that lake."

"Why?" said Frye. Her brown face was shrewd and placid in the gathering gloom. "You're afraid you died in that lake, aren't you?"

"Of course I'm not afraid of that! Aren't I standing right here talking to you?"

"You're afraid you drowned in that lake."

"Please, Frye, just keep your dumb mouth shut."

"That's what they thought, back there at the institution. You were in the water so long they assumed you were dead. There have been instances where individuals were submerged longer than you and yet they survived, but you were such a pitiful case to start with. A real dunderhead. Ugly as sin, too. That type never gets much consideration. They took one look at you after the grappling hook brought you up and they probably said, 'Horray, this poor, suffering soul is a goner!' Instead of really checking you out they turned you over to the space people. That was the way they always were, looking past you or around you but never straight at you, otherwise they might have noticed what a whopping mistake they made."

I knew she was right but I hated to admit it to myself. It must have happened the way she said. The pack in my head stimulated what few brain cells I possessed and made me more intelligent than I used to be. That didn't explain, though, how I seemed to be able to manipulate workers just as if I were wearing a hat.

"Your boyfriend is nuts, you know that, don't you?" said Frye.

"He isn't my boyfriend."

"Don't I know it? As far as he's concerned, you're a dead moose, but he brought us out here to kill us, sure as shootin'. I don't really mind for myself but I'm sorry about you."

"We'd better get out of here," I said. "If we stay here we'll freeze."

"What do you think we're going to do out there?" Frye turned to stare out at the tumbling snow.

"Come on, we've got to give it a try. I don't want to die on this planet. Earth is my place of birth and that's where I'll lay me down."

It was so cold my hair froze. I guess my bout of thinking had caused me to perspire and now I paid for it in the way the cruel air swooped upon me and made an icicle of every drop of moisture it found. The snow on the ground was hard so that we made crunching sounds as we walked along.

"I'll give you my shirt," said Frye.

"No, I can't bear the idea of your being naked. You keep it. Talk to me. Tell me about your mother."

"Those cells shut down when I died. Why do you keep opening them up?"

"I don't know. I care, Frye, I really do. Maybe I'm trying to understand everything in life."

"She was mean. Her deck was missing a few cards. Haywire chemistry; change-of-life psychosis that began when she was about thirty-five. There was no reasoning with her because she had a good intent behind everything she ever did, and justice was always on her side. She made my life a living hell."

I took hold of her when she stumbled, dragged her across a gully and got her feet going right again. The sky kept getting darker while the wind retained no sanity at all. It tried to tear my head off. "What about your father?" I said.

"I wrote him letters but his new wife tore them up. At night I slept under my bed with the door of my room locked. Finally she took an axe to it so after that I slept outside and sneaked in after she went to work."

"She was able to hold down a job?"

"Sure. Just about everything in her life was normal except where I was concerned. I don't know why and I don't think she knew, either, but all she wanted to do was kill me."

"What happened, finally?"

"Some neighbors took me in. I never saw her again but there wasn't a day I didn't think of her."

I sat down on the ground. "What a devil of a life you had. I'm sorry."

Frye looked around. "Is this where you want to do it? Are you laying down your life right here?"

"I can't go any farther. I'm too cold."

"This place isn't Earth. It's alien territory."

Getting up on my knees I stared into the distance. "I guess it won't care."

"If you die here you won't leave your mark anywhere."

"I left my mark plenty of places. Didn't I bring relief to a lot of people who were glad they weren't me? Didn't I teach my fellowman the virtues of compassion and pity?"

"That isn't enough. You have to get back there to the compound and watch out for Bates."

"I don't even like her."

"Yes, you do. You know she's the only decent one in that whole bunch. I think they must have gotten those people from jails or something."

"I'm in love with Peterkin," I said.

"I know, but he's the worst of all of them. Get up. You have a lot of walking to do."

I walked, or I tried to, and by and by I fell down and stayed there. Those frogs must have tuned in on my mental screams, otherwise they never would have found me in the darkness. It hurt them to carry me but they didn't want to take a chance trying to levitate me since they didn't often use their talents and weren't practiced at them. I was almost too heavy for them to haul. Then, too, they had to bring Frye along because I objected when they suggested leaving her behind.

They had a regular spa in their oasis, dunked me in a hot pool and fed me melons until I felt as if I was going to live. Felix was the frog who had been in the galley that day, and he remembered me. His real name was outlandish and he didn't mind my shortening it. He didn't mind anything I said or did. For the first time in my life I met somebody who truly liked me.

"How could I forget you?" he said. Frogs talked without using their mouths. Their thoughts came out of their heads loudly enough for me to hear them in my own head.

"How is Frye?" I needn't have asked. Humoring me, they had her in a pool, too, and were feeding her melons. The surprising thing was that they had done it while I was unconscious. Plainly they had the talent, too.

"Loneliness is not so bad with us," said Felix.

"That isn't why I kept her going," I said. "I just like her."

"She is no longer there. The shell is merely a puppet that you manipulate."

"Don't say that. She's real."

"Only in your mind. But if you don't wish us to speak of it, we won't."

While I recuperated he told me about the suffering of his people, how the expanding ice had destroyed their civilization and crippled their mental talents. Once they had lived without coming into physical contact with scarcely anything, but that was in their legends and they didn't actually remember. Other than during mating they seldom touched one another and then they only did it because of love.

"Now there are oases, iceland, hunger and waning talent," said Felix.

The oases weren't numerous or large enough for them to grow all the food they needed. There were fruit and melon trees, vegetable patches, a few flowers and a great deal of warm water. The frogs wanted one of the atomic engines from the oil compound.

"For what?" I said.

They knew that under the layers of ice their world was like the oases. With an engine they could clear enough acreage to have a farm. Literally they would burn away a patch of ice, right in this area where it was only a few yards thick, and they would keep it clear.

"It would mean our survival at least for a little while longer."

"Have you asked for the engine?" I said.

"Earthlings don't care if we die."

"Have they said as much?"

"They say they can't spare a machine."

Another reason Felix wanted the engine was for kan-alba, whatever that was.

All in all, there was far too much talk. Strangely satisfied and feeling accepted as just another person, I more or less fell asleep so that my hosts were compelled to haul me from the water before I went under. I forgot to ask them if they knew why I could manipulate the workers without a helmet. When I woke up I asked Felix and he said it was the machine in my head stimulating tissue that was normally inactive.

Chapter 8

Frogs were about five feet tall and weighed in the neighborhood of a hundred pounds. Not what you would call large people. They slept on beds of leaves that left their bodies sore and bruised. They might have been aquatic once but no one in the group remembered having heard the older ones mention it. Having depended upon the power of levitation and other mental abilities for so long, the species wasn't prepared for the ice and the cold that came when a comet tilted the planet's axis ever so slightly, and now their numbers had dwindled until there was practically nobody left.

"We think the ice may go as quickly as it came," said Felix. His mind spoke to my mind. "Our legends tell us that it will."

"If you could survive and hang on until that happens," I said.

"Yes, if only we could hang on."

The babies were little gray cuties with fine silken hair. Contact with things didn't seem to bother them. They clambered over people and other objects without wincing or groaning and I saw no raw patches on their skin. One climbed into my lap and I held it close. Never having been so near to a baby, I didn't know if this one smelled like a human. It was sweet and soft to the touch, intelligent looking and full of curiosity. Every now and then it took my face in its little hands and stared at me. It didn't make me uncomfortable, though I was unaccustomed to having anyone look directly at me. There were strange lights deep in the pools that illuminated the area and made it possible for me to see everything clearly.

"Do you think maybe you could get your special powers back to the full?" I asked Felix.

"Not as long as staying alive is so difficult. The talents require much concentration, full stomachs and sublime thought."

I made ready to leave, put my clothes back on and got Frye up off the ground. The frogs were all naked so I wasn't self-conscious. The only time they ever put anything on was when they went to my compatriots to beg.

Felix touched me on the arm and said, "If all Earthlings were like you we could do business with them."

The remark surprised me so much that I was unable to enlighten him. It might have been the first compliment I ever received. I couldn't tell him how I stacked up with other humans. Besides, he might not understand. Another besides: I was tired of always feeling down.

Land's End took twenty-six hours to turn on its axis, so Frye and I were able to make it back to the compound well before dawn. The doors were unlocked because the frogs never moved around at night and nobody else would ever try to get in. There were only the humans in the other compounds and their accommodations were much nicer than ours so they never bothered us. Wearing coats and hats Felix gave us from his cache and with his guidance, we returned home without much stress or strain.

Frye and I went through the hot and silent factory,

down the stairs to the living quarters, along a hall past a sleepy flunky on his way to the john. He was too out of it to really see us and did little more than mumble and stumble on past us.

I lay on my bunk thinking that I had to do something about LeMay. Really she was too much.

"You okay?" I asked Frye. She gave me not so much as a grunt. "How about you?" I said to Zott.

"I wish you'd leave my memory cells alone. They're none of your business."

The place settled down and I listened to my heart pump. LeMay, stinking up the place, kept me from concentrating on getting to sleep. Her hand wasn't healing either. That morning I had checked it out and it looked the same. I didn't think it would ever change, and in fact I doubted if anything about her would ever be any different, other than her smell. That could only get worse.

Then I remembered the perfume on the counter in the cafeteria where the cooks ladled out the chow. Immediately I hopped out of bed and went into the hall where it was empty and dark, cold and quiet. I hated darkness but turning on the lights down here among the dead could only get me into trouble so I felt along the walls and made my way upstairs.

The perfume wasn't on the counter. I felt the areas beside the empty food bins and along the dessert cases but there were no bottles of perfume, only catsup, mustard, salt and pepper. Which reminded me that Mildred was too light with the salt so I slipped a cellar into my pocket. Feeling my way along the counter to my left, I found the swinging gate and went into the serving area. Inside the kitchen itself I had to have some light. No way could I find anything among the huge pots, jutting stoves and counters. I flipped every switch in the room. Just as I was about to begin my search, someone came through the swinging gate in the serving area.

"I'm sick of you lousy flunkies sneaking in here at night and stealing me blind!" said a testy voice that I recognized. "They only give me so many supplies and I can't stretch them far enough the way it is! This time I'll know who the thief is and I'll have you canned!"

Mildred came barging through the door into the kitchen behind me, immediately stopped and made a loud whooshing sound as if someone had slugged her in the belly. I turned all the way around to look at her. Her mouth a round O, she leaned back against the door sill, one hand clutching her throat, the other spread across an ample breast. She had buggy light eyes and her stringy red hair was wrapped in curlers that dangled over her forehead like monstrous bangs. She needed to lose about thirty pounds and at the moment all her excess was wobbling. As I stood there looking at her, I wondered if she was going to scream.

She didn't look as if she would ever breathe again, leaned back against the door sill as if she intended staying there forever, which was all right with me. Just before she came in I had spotted the bottle of perfume on a shelf along with some other cosmetics, so now I made my way between two rows of washtubs, reached out and plucked it up. After that I helped myself to a loaf of bread and a sack of cheese. Then I turned and walked past my petrified audience, giving her a wink as I did so.

I don't know what was going through her mind. As big as I was, I could still walk without sound when I wanted to, and as I moved toward the exit I heard absolutely nothing coming from the kitchen. Mildred must have been frozen in her position by the door. I wondered if she would be there at dinnertime tomorrow.

The perfume made LeMay smell better but only after I dumped a quarter of it on my own shirt. Putting it on my roommate didn't improve anything. With the sweet odor clogging my nostrils, I ate the bread and cheese, with the realization that I couldn't really enjoy the food when I was unable to smell it.

Sometime toward morning I forgave Peterkin for having tried to murder me. He hadn't been guilty of anything other than attempting to rid himself of a couple of ugly nuisances. Not that Frye was so hard to look at. Her brown skin looked somewhat ashen, though, and there was no way of ignoring the big dark rings circling her eyes. Her lips were a bit pale, too. Come to think of it, she looked pretty bad but that was only until I compared her in my mind to myself. Then she came out ahead.

Obviously Peterkin was beset by devils that seemed to be part and parcel with mortality, so I forgave him for leaving me out on the ice. Now I only hoped he would forgive me and not think up any more drastic adventures for me.

I didn't see him all that day and had begun to relax until we went to the cafeteria for dinner and I remembered Mildred. Her eyes were raw sores glaring at me from her chalky face. Standing behind the mashed potato bin, she stared across the counter at me as if she saw an apparition. There I was, as big as life, or whatever she called it, and she looked more like a stiff than the stiffs in line beside me. White face, numb lips that tried to smile, she was scared witless, but she was careful to give me plenty to eat. With painful exactness she ladled out the spuds in their proper hole in my tray, a couple of foot-long steaks were laid underneath a mountain of Jell-o, cake, peas, onions, salad and ice cream. It looked good only to me.

I winked and nodded at her but her look of horror just increased and I don't think she breathed until we were all finished eating and were on our way out the door. I know because I watched her the whole time. Maybe she didn't tell on me because she figured nobody would believe her that a stiff could be independent. They might decide she had finally flipped her lid and book her a passage on the next shuttle to Earth. Or maybe the terror in her situation fed a warped kind of need. The goings-on in Land's End required fortitude on the part of the participants. Mildred might be like all the other living people I had met here so far. She couldn't cope in an ordinary way so she did the next best thing. She did whatever she had to do in order not to blow her cork; she accepted the unacceptable. That was fine with me because it meant that every time I went into the cafeteria I received red-carpet treatment. I was the best-fed worker in the joint.

It was when we were leaving that Peterkin spotted us. He saw Frye coming out into the hall on her way downstairs. He didn't look as if he believed what he was seeing but then his eyes went hunting for me in the crowd, and there I was sticking up a foot higher than everyone else. He wasn't nearly as transparent as Mildred and kept most of his emotions hidden but I could tell he was stunned. After observing him for so long, I had learned to read him fairly accurately. He was dismayed, shocked, scared and reeling with confusion. Mostly, though, he was enraged to see Frye and me safely back at our posts. If ever there was a man who hated to be crossed, it was he.

Chapter 9

Quidler wore the driver's hat with us in the galley the next day. He was a man who never enjoyed his work and wore an expression that said he couldn't wait for a different tour of duty. I don't know whether he was several steps above the flunkies or just another low-paid employee of the mining company. He didn't wear a special uniform, just the ordinary blue pants and shirt everybody wore, but now and then he acted more disciplined than most. Except when he was trying to make points with Bates or when he was quarreling with Peterkin.

In his mid-twenties, he had short stiff brown hair and a big nose; not that he was unattractive but he wasn't tall and handsome like Peterkin. He didn't mind lording it over us workers but he didn't like kitchen work.

"You people aren't people at all and you can't even

follow simple directions!" he said to us. Actually he was glaring at Zott who kept fiddling with his belt. "Even if you had brains inside your brains you'd be dumb! I don't want any gold-bricking. I want you to hustle those garbage tubs out to the incinerator on the double and I want the contents dumped without any spilling. No mixups! A plain and simple chore done right!"

It wasn't such a simple chore because Zott, Frye and LeMay kept doing distracting things. I know it was my fault but I was grumpy and bored.

"This stinking helmet is on the fritz again!" Quidler fumed, looking as if he was tempted to take off the hat and examine it, but if he did that everyone would fall down. Speaking aloud to Zott he said, "Leave your belt alone! Do only what I tell you! Help that big clod next to you pick up the nearest tub! Do it!"

Zott wrapped his arms around the tub and tried lifting it but it wouldn't come off the table until I helped. As soon as Quidler turned his attention elsewhere, Zott let go so that the tub slammed back down.

"Holy smoke, get down at the other end of the room. You smell like a grave!" Quidler yelled at LeMay, his face screwing up into a big scowl. "This place is nuts!" he said. "They make us work with corpses, and I can see some logic in the idea, but do they have to be ripe?"

Taking a notebook and pencil from his pocket, he wrote down LeMay's description. She had no name, no number, no identifying mark of any kind. What she was was a dum-dum, the lowest form of existence in reality anywhere. Even a post had more personality than LeMay, or so Quidler told her as loudly as he could.

"If they don't get these stinking helmets fixed I'm gonna blow my brains out!" he said. "You, there, what the devil do you think you're doing? Stop that!" Frye was digging down into a tub with one hand. She didn't pay any attention to him, kept diving down into the beef stew until she was up to her shoulder.

While he was having a fit over such insubordination, LeMay came up to him, took off the glove I had given her and showed him her wounded hand. It didn't smell any worse than the rest of her but it looked terrible, like a big pink and blue bruise. Behind her, Zott took off his belt and commenced stringing himself up on an overhead beam.

"That's not a bad idea," said Frye and made as if to climb into the tub. "I think I'll drown myself in this soup."

"I can't stand it!" Quidler said in a loud voice. "You're doing this on purpose! You're trying to drive me crazy! What do you want, blood?"

"What the devil is all the racket about?" said Peterkin from the doorway. "With all your noise you scared the cooks into running away before they finished in the kitchen. Who's going to wash these tubs after they're dumped?"

"Who cares?" said Quidler. "If I told these idiots to do it, they'd just ignore me. Look at them! I want you to look at what they're doing and tell me if I'm seeing things!"

With an expression of mild annoyance, Peterkin scrutinized all of us. "Well? Well?"

There was nothing for him to comment about because we weren't doing anything. Zott had his belt back on and was standing still with an unintelligent stare; LeMay was wearing her glove again, while Frye stood, dripping stew down her arm onto the floor.

"They're doing it on purpose," said Quidler. "They're doing all kinds of stuff. I'm telling you, this stinking helmet is fractured!"

Peterkin came on into the room, walked past LeMay, immediately wrinkled up his nose and peered into a tub. "What's that stink? Don't tell me we ate this stuff for dinner! It's rotten!"

"Why can't we have decent equipment? They tell us how essential this dump is to Earth's economy and they spend all that money on packs for these airheads and then they buy cheap fuses and wiring for the hats!"

"Never mind all that." Peterkin must have just gotten

out of the shower because his hair was still damp. Fresh and pretty as a picture, his clothes looking newly laundered and his skin glowing, he said, "I want to know why you followed me out on the ice last night and brought back those two dum-dums?"

"What two dum-dums?"

"You know very well which two. That big one over there and the tan female."

"What are you talking about?" Quidler was beginning to look and sound cranky.

"You know very well what I'm talking about."

"No, I don't. Why can't you answer simple questions instead of asking stupid ones?"

Peterkin frowned. "Who paid you to do it? Shirley? She wouldn't do that."

"Why don't you dry up and get lost?"

"Would she pay you?" Thoughtfully Peterkin studied his shoes. "Would she stoop so low? Is it that important to her to make me look bad?"

"You're psycho, you know that, don't you? Shirley can't stand the sight of you so she doesn't give a hang how you look. Why don't you get on out of here like a nice little creep and let me do my work?"

"I've had about enough of your insulting mouth." Peterkin advanced another step or two, his expression no longer amiable and condescending. In fact, it had gone unfriendly and even hostile.

"Oh, yeah?" Quidler yelled. Unnerved by things he couldn't explain or rationalize, he took some quick steps of his own toward the other man. Peterkin was bigger than he but not nearly so hard and was not in condition. "Oh, yeah? Is that so? Come to think of it, I got a yen to punch you in your psychotic lip! Come on, come on!"

Frye tipped over her tub, spilling beef stew all over the floor. Quidler had been about to take a swing at Peterkin but now he lost his balance and fell on his knees. Peterkin was in the act of backing out of the battle arena in a hurry. He too slipped on a slab of meat and landed on his rear.

Tubs started tipping all the way down the line of tables and workers slid this way and that, skated to maintain their equilibrium, some falling, others trying to obey the skitzy commands issuing from the helmet on Quidler's head. So intent was he on getting through the soup to land one on Peterkin's mug that the desire was transferred to the workers. They began swinging fists left and right, punching out anybody and everybody near them.

Not in the mood for a brawl, I picked up a full tub and carried it outside where Felix and a group of frogs were waiting.

"I hate to dump this on the ground," I said. "It doesn't seem decent for you to eat that way. Besides, it's soup and most of it will soak in before you can get it."

Not to worry, Felix and his friends had a solution to the problem. "Put it down, please," he said.

The tub weighed a couple of hundred pounds and began sinking in the snow as soon as I let go of it. It didn't get too far before eight or nine more frogs ran up and made funny lifting motions with their hands. They didn't touch the container with their bodies but only with their minds.

I watched in admiration as the big smoking can came up out of the hole in the snow, easy as pie. Squinting, frowning, concentrating, staring, the little people kept making the same lifting motions. Four on each side and one behind, they slowly walked across the ice away from the building, leaving pink tracks behind them as they made away with enough food to feed their tribe for a week.

Back inside, the galley was a mess. Some flunkies had dragged Quidler and Peterkin off to the brig in the basement while a fuzzy-chinned kid had the helmet on his head and was trying to drive. He saw me coming in the door and his eyes popped.

"Stand there!" he yelled at me. "Don't come any closer!"

I did what he wanted, did this, did that, followed every little mindless direction he gave me until he was confident

that I was under his control and wasn't going to jump
him. He was one of the more superstitious types. Show
him an upright corpse and his imagination just naturally
made unholy assumptions.

Do this, do that, everyone tried doing what he wanted
but there had been a lot of grease in Mildred's stew and
the footing was less than reliable.

It was late when we got to bed that night.

Chapter 10

I lay in my bunk trying to solve a puzzle. Considering
expense in hard money, did it cost more to make a robot
worker or a worker like, say, Zott? A robot worker cost
about fifty thousand dollars while Zott cost two thousand,
half for the pack and half for the surgery. The robot
didn't bother anybody while Zott bothered everybody. If a
person walked around a corner and came face to face
with a robot, he might look to see if the thing was going
to behave and then he went on about his business. Meet-
ing Zott around a corner, particularly a dark one, could be
a hazardous experience. So in the long run, which cost the
most?

"You don't like me," said Zott. He was staring at the
wall.

"Why wouldn't I like you?" I said.

"Because I killed that guy. They gave me a terminal
hypo for doing it, you know."

I shrugged. "I'm not sure how I feel about killing. I
mean, I don't know whether to feel sorry for murderers or
to have utter contempt for them."

"Couldn't you ever kill anyone?"

"Certainly not calmly and coolly."

"How about in a fit of passion?"

I thought about it. "I've never been mad enough to kill, so far in my life. Oh, I've been mad but I was always able to walk away without committing any violence."

LeMay spoke up. "My life isn't a matter of discussion. In other words, my memories are my own business."

"I want to die," said Frye. "I hope someone stops me before I kill my daughter. Ah, that's right, I forgot, I stopped myself."

"Hey, are you getting yourself confused with your mother?" said Zott.

Hanging over the top bunk, Frye looked down at him. "That I would never do. Those years after I finally escaped from home are clear in my mind but my adulthood is a blur. Except for the worst part of it."

"Which part is that?"

"I had the same thing my mother had. The same sickness. It came on me in my thirties. I don't remember anything except one night when I came to my senses and found myself chopping my daughter's bedroom door with an axe. My mind was so clear all of a sudden and I knew what was happening. I was doing the same thing to my daughter that my mother did to me. My baby was in her bedroom screaming while I was trying to get in to kill her."

"That's bad," said Zott. "I hope you didn't succeed."

"As soon as I realized what I had become and what I was doing, I went out into the kitchen and sliced my wrists with a butcher knife."

"That's bad," said Zott.

We didn't talk anymore after that. I don't know what my roommates did but I fell asleep, had nightmares and awakened in the morning when Bates drove us out of bed.

We worked in the factory that day and my face blistered again. They didn't care about our feelings. Only machines were fit to labor in the vicinity of that vat yet here we were, flesh and blood slaves, forced to do it. More than one worker stumbled or fell if he got too close to the bubbling metal for too long a period. Whenever a person's brain began to heat, the pack malfunctioned, forcing Bates to send in a flunky to haul him to a corner until he recovered.

I made it a point to avoid the vat. It was a terrifying spectacle for me to have to look at all the time. I kept thinking about what it would be like to fall into the bubbling cauldron.

Bates kept a close eye on Zott because she still wasn't certain his pack functioned properly. Since Peterkin and Quidler were still in the brig in the basement, she had only flunkies to give her a hand and to run errands.

It didn't matter because she wasn't planning to do much work that day, anyhow. Her husband had written her a letter telling her that it was nice if she wanted to have a career and make lots of money but he didn't intend waiting until her tour of duty here was finished. He had met someone else and was filing for divorce. Bates read the letter a hundred times and then proceeded to get bombed out of her skull.

We workers knew all this because she told us every detail several times over the microphone. We made some pretty weird looking bars and hooks that afternoon. I remember it vividly because it was the only time the vat didn't scare me. Toward afternoon Bates had everything turned off, including the heating of the vat, so that the metal turned black and no longer bubbled. I wondered if it felt cool but my curiosity wasn't strong enough to lead me to try to find out.

The first inkling we had that anything was out of the ordinary was when she told everybody to stop what they were doing and look up at her. We could see her plainly behind the glass, about twenty feet over our heads. The booth was twenty feet wide, full of machinery and cabinets.

She read us the letter and told us all about how she hated men because they couldn't rise above their threatened ego and accept women as something other than sex objects. There was no use trying to be friends with them or have a business relationship with them because they were conditioned like Pavlov's dog, and as soon as they spotted an attractive female they started drooling.

She must have guzzled a quart of redeye while she sat up there blubbering and telling us what was on her mind. "None of this is your business but I'm telling you anyway because you're the only friends I've got!" she said into the mike. She stood swaying like a drunkard, which is what she was that day. "You poor souls belong in the ground back on Earth," she said. "My heart yearns for you to have your rest but nobody back there listens to me. They're a gaggle of pismires who never grew up, pretending to be scientific, but their real motive is to do things that give people horrifying little jolts."

Eventually everything shut down but by then we didn't notice, we were so busy carousing. She had a pretty good voice and sang a song somebody had pirated from one of the old masters. Under her tutelage we all chose partners down in the factory and waltzed between the machines.

"I don't care if you never do another lick of work on this lousy planet!" said Bates, during a lull of her own making. We stayed close to our partners and waited for the next move. Sometimes she was more in the mood for talk than action. "You did your work during your lifetime!" she said, emphasizing the last word with a hiccup. "They have no morals! They have no right doing this to you. Aren't you worth more than this? You were mothers and fathers, husbands and wives, sons and daughters and a lot of people loved you. Now they have you walking around like a bunch of ghosts doing work monkeys can do! I tell you, it's a sin!" Hiccup.

On into the evening we danced and I don't know what the cooks must have thought. Maybe they were used to it. One of them came to the factory door, looked in, made the sign of the cross and hastily withdrew. I guess it wasn't a first for Bates, this retreat from mundane existence. No flunkies showed up to object, in fact nobody showed up. There was only the broken-hearted lady in her glass booth with her metal hat and jug of redeye, and there we were, all us poor souls, dancing to whatever tune our inebriated driver cared to sing.

After a while she settled for "Waltzing Matilda." I had heard it before and especially liked the sorrow and sadness it evoked within me. It was all about recklessness in the face of disaster, love that had died, sad memory. I knew all about the last part, never having had any other kind.

"She's going to come pitching down through that glass one of these times," Zott said to me.

"Belay that talking!" Bates said. "Workers don't talk. Everyone knows that. Workers don't think. They don't do anything. They belong in the ground."

"With the worms," said Frye. "That song makes me want to sniffle." She did.

Tears spilling down her cheeks, Bates leaned her forehead on the glass and stared down at us. "Did I ever tell you how much I hate men?" she said. "They think we women are always wondering about them but they're wrong. Folks have to be interesting to attract sustained attention." She gave the glass partition a whack with the bottle. "I wish I'd never been born," she said. "I particularly hate the postal service that delivers letters."

I was climbing up the wall under the booth, using ledges for handholds, when she hit the glass hard enough to crack it. Shards rained down around me but luckily I didn't get cut or knocked off my perch.

"I want to sing some more!" she said as I climbed in. "I want everybody to dance!"

She was so bombed out of her mind, I could have been Dracula and she never would have known the difference. Emptying the bottle with a final gulp, she stuffed her Dear John letter in the neck and sent it flying across the room where it landed in the vat. The metal only looked cool, sucked the bottle downward in a flash and a little puff of smoke was all that was left of Bates' last farewell from her husband.

She wasn't done by a long shot. First she made me sit

down, after which she fitted the helmet on my head. Then she conducted a silent orchestra while I directed the low-lies in a graceful waltz. Matilda had a real workout that night.

One thing she shouldn't have done was get a second bottle from the cabinet. Another thing that oughtn't to have happened was that she gave me a nip or three. I had never had a drink before and the stuff hit me like a ton of bricks. The last thing I remembered was dismantling the booth and tossing it across space into the vat.

Forever after that, for as long as she lived, Bates never looked at me without a little frown on her face, as if she were trying to remember something.

"You were a one-woman disaster," said LeMay the next day. She was speaking of my drunken night out.

"I already apologized for that. Don't keep reminding me."

"As if that will make us forget. You nearly gave yourself away, you know. If Bates hadn't been so far gone, she would remember."

I shrugged. "I saw her this morning and she didn't seem different."

"Because she feels lousy and can't recall."

They had already told me all about it. That was an advantage to having a weird talent like mine. My conscious mind had lost the events of that night but my unconscious revealed them to me via my fractured communications with my companions.

I hadn't been all that bad, became exuberant to a dangerous degree but only tore up the booth and some of the machines I didn't like. Bates and I had a brawl because she wanted the metal hat back, but I won because she was so small.

"She remembers you had a big part in the destruction," said Frye. "Personally I think she believes she drove you up into the booth and forced you to break things. In my opinion your position is secure. Whatever it is."

"She remembers me talking," I said. "I'm pretty sure. I

talked a lot. More than I ever talked to anyone. I told her all about the institution."

Frye looked concerned. "Did you tell her about how they used to boot you around?"

"Yeah."

"About how they starved you?"

"Yeah."

Scratching her head she said, "There's one good thing about a drunken stupor. Reality has a way of blending in with pink elephants."

Chapter 11

On the night Peterkin sneaked into my room he had a flunky with him. I guess he hadn't the nerve to come alone. They turned on the lights because there were no windows in the place and nobody would notice.

"There's something wrong with one of these stiffs," Peterkin said in a low voice.

The flunky was young and ignorant, one of the many kids who left their homeworld with exaggerated dreams of getting rich in the mines in the sky. "Which one?" he said.

"That's just it. I don't know."

"What's wrong with the special one?"

"That's another thing I don't know." Peterkin stood by the bunks and looked at each one of us in turn.

The flunky made a gasping sound. "I can tell you what's wrong with that one!" he said, backing away from LeMay.

"What?"

"Is there something wrong with your nose?"

"You mean the stink? They all smell ripe to me."

"No, it's only her. I know the reason, too. Her tissues are rejecting the pack they put in her head."

Peterkin moved over to LeMay, his nose wrinkling. "She's driven like the others. She does her work."

"I don't see how. I worked in pack surgery and only rejectors smelled this bad. Hers must have been a delayed reaction for her to get all the way here and be put on the job."

"What's going to happen?"

The kid looked at Peterkin as if he had gone simple. "Haven't you ever heard of the law of nature?" He moved toward the door.

"Wait a minute, don't let your precious sense of aesthetics keep you from your duty. I paid you to help me find out what's wrong with this miserable quartet."

"I just did. One of them is rotting like a side of beef."

"That can't have anything to do with—" Peterkin didn't bother to finish because the flunky was already out the door and hurrying down the hall. He stood looking after the youth, muttering under his breath about dire consequences for welching punks. Finally he came back inside and stood staring at LeMay. "Can that be it?" he said aloud. "But how could her dead brain's refusing to be activated by a pack affect the behavior of these other baboons?" His expression brightened. "Whatever it is, it's something weird. Maybe she is the cause of it. Why not?"

Seeming much cheered, he went away to the boss to report LeMay's condition. Bates had recuperated from her hangover but she wasn't interested in shortening the work force by getting rid of LeMay. There couldn't be anything wrong with the stiff. She was doing her job, wasn't she? Enraged because he couldn't have his way, Peterkin still took the time to make a pass at her and was spurned. No matter what he did he always seemed to strike out.

"You don't even talk to me!" he said. "You talk to Quidler! What's the difference between him and me?"

"He takes no for an answer."

I knew all this had taken place because the cooks discussed it while they ladled out food at suppertime.

"That's the one," said one of them, pointing at us. "She's the one causing the bad smell."

I could see how quickly Mildred perked up. Eagerly she looked in my direction, only to appear crestfallen when she discovered the target was LeMay and not me. No doubt she longed for any kind of explanation for me and was willing to grasp at straws.

"What a shame!" said another cook. "Cut down in her prime, she can't even live the life of a stiff! I can't tell if anything is off color about her, what with the smell of these onions going up my nose. If it's true, though, won't she begin to lose her looks?"

"As if she has any now!" someone said. "You've been up here too long, honey. Better apply for R and R."

It was several days before we went back into the factory because the glass booth had to be rebuilt and the broken machines needed to be replaced. I didn't mind painting walls and pulling galley duty. At least there was no bubbling vat to blister the skin on my nose.

But then work returned to normal and we filed into the hot box like a bunch of somnambulists, one by one, answering the call of Bates who sat up in her new booth with the metal hat on her head.

My companions were never too graceful because the packs in their brains weren't attached to enough nerve endings. They were also dead, so what could one expect? Refugees from execution chambers and morgues, accident victims, suicides, the unclaimed—and one unfortunate who didn't know if she was half dead or half alive. It was still okay. I never had much sense, though I wasn't the lamebrain the doctors insisted I was, but I knew enough to realize I was probably better off here than back in the institution. I was tired of being a guinea pig and a specimen for psychology students to come and view during class outings.

I had as many feelings as anyone. I also had a bit of intuition, so that when Bates was due to report to hospital for her annual physical and Peterkin showed up to fill in as driver for her, I experienced a sense of disquiet.

"What are you doing here?" Bates said in her chilliest tone. Too chilly, in my opinion. The microphone was turned on and I could hear their conversation.

"Hey, it's all right," said Peterkin. "Quidler is under the weather, is all."

"You mean you bribed him. Anything for an ulterior motive, if you ask me."

"You've got me all wrong. I'm merely trying to get on the good side of you. After all, you guarantee my bread and butter."

"No, I don't. If I did you'd be out of work. But the first time someone with half a mind volunteers to come here, you'll be on the return flight out." Bates utilized the automatic computer to keep all us workers tuned in and on our feet while she transferred the driver's hat. In a few minutes she was gone and we were left at the beck and call of Peterkin.

I think he was burning because of her remarks. Do this, do that, and we didn't need so numerous and such exact directions. He was all over the factory with his mind, but not smoothly and not intently. Rather his thinking was erratic and poorly focused so that the workers began making jerky little motions like the characters in an old silent film.

Zott got up from his machine and stretched. Peterkin roared at him to sit down, which he did.

"That guy reminds me of a slaver," said Frye to me. "I know you like him but you've never been renowned for your good taste or judgment."

LeMay whammed hot blocks with a hammer and tried not to hit her hand. "I don't care what he does," she said. "As far as I'm concerned, he's just another pretty face."

I felt Peterkin trying to maneuver the four of us and I resisted. I could tell it made him mad by the way he stood up and began bellowing into the mike. It wasn't there for communication between us and the driver but was strictly for summoning flunkies and directing them down in the work area. Peterkin didn't care, yelled at us through the instrument as though we had ears that heard.

"You birdbrains will do exactly as you're told and I don't mean yesterday!" he yelled. "You there, you idiot at the vertical sealer, stand up and get away from that machine."

"That guy is sick," said Zott, but he did as he was told, stood up and wandered away, and since Peterkin didn't tell him to stop he continued walking until he came up against a wall.

While I was wondering why Peterkin had done such a thing, he ordered Frye to go over to the next machine and hit the operator on the head with a greasy rag. Meanwhile he was urging me to go stand in a corner. Instead I went over to Frye and asked her what she thought she was doing. Unfortunately I forgot all about LeMay.

"I'm only doing what I was told," said Frye, hitting the stiff over and over again with the rag. It was big and heavy and soaked with grease. The man paid no attention to her, operated his machine as if all were ordinary. Since it wasn't, his performance wasn't of the best. One of his shirt buttons caught in a metal maw and he was dragged down until his chin came up hard against a pair of rollers.

"Now look what you've done!" I said to Frye. "How's he going to get out of that?"

"You fix it."

I looked around to see if Peterkin was watching but his attention was drawn elsewhere. Quickly I forced the jaws of the maw open with my bare hands, settled the stiff into his chair and then led Frye back to her machine. "Sit there and do your job, no matter what he tells you," I said. "Don't get up and don't pay any attention to him."

Why the diversive tactics on Peterkin's part I didn't know. He possessed a good understanding of brain packs so maybe he was simply protecting himself. For all he knew there might be cameras hidden on one or two of us and he didn't want any photographs of what he was about to do. Actually I doubt if he feared any such thing but was merely rendered irrational by a bad conscience. It

was habit with him. Practically everything he did was pro-
hibited by one law or another so that he continually
worried about getting caught.

While everyone was occupied, he ordered LeMay to
leave her post and climb the rails above the vat. They
hadn't been built to be scaled but were supports for the
pot into which chunks of solid metal were fed. There were
tubes leading out of the container through which the
melted metal flowed. The struts were thick and wide and
formed a kind of webbing near the ceiling high over the
bubbling mass.

LeMay probably absorbed too much damage as soon as
she got close to the vat. The tremendous heat no doubt
set her blood to boiling and rendered her brain incapable
of sustaining the pack embedded in it. Or vice versa. The
last comprehensible command she received was the one
from the driver telling her to climb the webbing. Conflict-
ing orders that came later went in one ear and out the
other. After I finally turned around and saw what was
happening I tried to stop her but she was too far gone.

The web directly over the center of the vat, about sixty
feet up, was where she finally came to a halt. With a sigh
which was most likely the last of the tidal air being ex-
pelled from her lungs, she lay on her stomach across the
metal struts and looked down. The bones already showed
in her hands where they had come in contact with hot
steel. Her shirt and pants turned bright yellow and began
to burn, not swiftly but slowly, the low flames curling and
turning the fabric black. At the same time her face turned
scarlet while the hair burned on her head. Her shoes
curled and fell off. She roasted like a pig on a spit but not
nearly as slowly and far more thoroughly. The stink of
burned flesh filled the factory. Fat dripped in steady
streams, organs swelled and burst, muscles slid off bones
as if they were liquid. The terrible heat from the vat
swooped upward and cleaned my friend's skeleton more
thoroughly than a pack of buzzards could have done it.
She was so little, way up there, so insignificant, so unno-
ticeable.

Bates came back and took over as driver but saw nothing out of the ordinary because she wasn't in the habit of looking at the vat. Nobody was; that was how awesome and menacing it was. Peterkin walked out of the booth with a satisfied little smile on his face and I was left sitting at my machine trying not to stare up at what was left of my one-time friend.

Of course they noticed her eventually, but not until several days had passed, not until a flunky with restless eyes who didn't like looking at us glanced up and spotted the gleaming skeleton lying on the webbing. All they cared was that they had discovered what happened to the missing worker.

Bates didn't tie it in with Peterkin. Both he and Quidler had spelled her several times over the past days, besides which, she couldn't imagine why anyone would want to murder a stiff. Neither could anyone else. Only Peterkin was aware of his motive.

They brought us a new roommate named Flora, an old and gray-haired woman who had died of a broken heart. At least that's what she told me. The flunkies who delivered her became nervous because our beds were made.

"I've been here too long," one said, sweating as he looked at us and our clean linen. He was young and blond, a pretty kid who didn't belong here. Earth should have found him a good job instead of encouraging him to leave his homeworld.

The other was also young, freckled, gray of complexion, scared out of his wits. "I haven't been here long enough," he said. "Since when do they have sheets on their beds and things like people?"

"Since never," said Blondie. "Only in this room. It's got a jinx on it. They say the king of the frogs made vapor of himself and lives in the walls."

Freckles shoved Flora all the way into the top bunk and backed away. "What's he doing in the walls?"

"Waiting to take his revenge on humans for not melting the snow on this planet."

"If you ask me he's already had his revenge. This place turns my blood to ice."

"Especially this room," said Blondie. "Don't expect it to be like the other rooms and don't expect the stiffs to be like the others. At least the one that stunk is gone. She climbed on the slats above the vat and melted like wax."

The freckles on Freckle's face seemed to have faded, so pale was he. "Why aren't these stiffs like all the others?"

"Some say they're haunted with the ghosts of frogs."

Freckles beat it out the door and down the hall. Following him out, Blondie chuckled. Slowly he came back and stared in at us. He ceased his chuckling, shook his head and went away, looking sober and even pessimistic.

Chapter 12

"Will you kindly stop comparing me with LeMay?" said Flora. "I'm another person. You make her sound like a paragon of all that's good." The old lady had done a hard day's work in the factory and wasn't in a congenial mood.

"Don't get testy," said Zott. "I was just beginning to think we might be friends."

"What does that mean?"

"That I hate women and it's a rare female I feel like taking to my bosom."

"Literally?"

"Not by a long shot. But I hate 'em literally. They carry us in their wombs and give us hormones to grow up and love attractive dames but when we do we get our throats cut."

"Literally?" said Flora.

Zott go so mad he yelled and swore and finally turned to the wall, refusing to talk or answer so much as a single additional question.

"You don't love Peterkin anymore, do you?" Flora said to me.

I was annoyed because she was being overly familiar for someone who had been our roommate such a short time.

"Just exactly what are you feelings now?" she said.

"None of your business." I didn't know how I felt about Peterkin. Mostly I was confused because I wasn't sure what crime he was guilty of. After all, I could only reason with suppositions. Had LeMay been alive and well, then what Peterkin did to her could be classified as cold blooded murder. As it was, though, what was it?

The sheets were dirty so I went down the hall to collect a fresh supply of linen. I was in a bad mood and didn't care if I was seen. Furthermore, if a flunky did see me and said so much as boo, I'd toss him through a wall. No one saw me, though, and I didn't know if I was glad about it or sorry. Leaving the dirty linen on the floor by the closet, I took the fresh stuff back to the room and bullied my associates into doing their beds.

"This is dumb, you know," said Frye. "Half the time I forget to take off my boots before I go to bed."

"See that you remember after this. You're a slob if you don't make your bed at least once a month."

"Who said so? One of the doctors at the institution?"

"That's none of your business." I didn't want to think about that. I had never wanted to think about it, not even when it was happening; or especially then. It was bad enough to be big and dumb and ugly but it was worse when you were perfectly aware of it. Some people came out of the womb hale, hearty and comely, and then there were others who came out like me. The little dangling chains of life material in the chromosomes of a developing embryo sometimes sustained damage, in which case it was difficult to predict what the baby was going to look like when it was born. I didn't have any say about what I looked like but if I had, I'd have looked like Bates.

Being in such a bad mood, thinking about LeMay's skeleton stuck up there on the webbing above the vat for so many days, grinning down with her teeth and bones, thinking about my misfortune in having been born, I was restless and couldn't sleep. Most of the night I prowled and paced in the room, back and forth, from wall to wall, kicking whatever got in my way. I was in a dilemma, trying to make a decision about something.

Once during the night someone was disturbed in the flunkies' quarters and came part way down the hall but then chickened out and went back where he belonged. They were always doing that so I paid no attention. Those flunkies were all babies and belonged back home with their families. Forever they were creeping down the dark hallway to see why we stiffs made so much noise. Maybe they expected us to lie like frozen slabs from dark to dawn; maybe they never considered that one of their fancy doctors could make a dreadful mistake and try to turn a dumbbell into a mindless idiot. I wasn't mindless but at the moment I was cranky, and if any flunky showed his face in my territory I'd toss him through a wall.

Toward morning I made up my mind about the problem, turned out the light and entered the darkened hallway. Up the stairs and along some more corridors to the kitchen I went, not that it was my ultimate destination. It was just that I remembered the dinner we'd had and realized I was still hungry.

Weird Mildred was in the pots and pans section, skulking behind a counter like a refugee from an asylum. I think she was beginning to enjoy her maniacal state. She must have since she could have remained in her room nights instead of sneaking up to her kitchen to see if her favorite stiff was abroad. She never spoke but took a horrified stance and watched while I plundered in the cabinets and refrigerators. Plenty of times she could have locked me in one of the freezers but she never stirred, just crouched against the wall and waited to see what I was going to do. In a way I felt sorry for her. Poor, homely, alive old bag, unwanted by anybody, obviously, else why would she take such a job.

Fortified with a batch of chicken, I quit the kitchen and headed for the galley out back. It was dark there and the big empty cans caught reflections through the window from the snow outside. There was a tiny moon overhead, a white ball in a cloudy sky but it was light enough so that I could see the frogs. They kept sentries posted outside in case somebody came to give them food. Nobody ever did that at night so I wondered why they went to the trouble of standing in freezing snow in the dark, but they always did it. It wasn't that they were stupid. In fact they were highly intelligent. They were just hungry.

Did any of it make any sense? If the frogs' diet improved they might keep their species going for a few centuries until the glaciers moved off to the poles and the ground became more amiable to seeds. I mean, why bother? If life wasn't enjoyable what was it good for? Why not just fade away into extinction without complaining?

Felix and his friends were grateful for the food. They invited me to eat with them but I was full and not feeling cheerful so I repaired to the edge of the oasis and sat watching the moon. No romantic tunes would ever be inspired by that chill little lamp. Half a million miles distant, niggardly was a good description of its friendliness.

The oasis was half a mile square with some tropical jungle, hot pools, arid land, fruit trees and small furry animals. The frogs always ate any meat they could get their hands on but they never killed the animals on their little islands. They had no weapons that I could see. Something else I couldn't see was how such a sublime species had managed to last so long.

Had the colonists from Earth asked permission to build their camps and factories? Not likely. In the first place they couldn't distinguish one frog from another and didn't know who the leader was, and in the second place they were accustomed to dealing with inferior lifeforms on other worlds. They didn't kill anyone on those alien planets but simply shoved them aside to make room for their buildings and machinery.

While I waited at the oasis, I saw something I didn't understand. One of the furry animals was dying, an old one I guessed from the look of it. The fur was short and skimpy and there was a grizzled look about the face. It weighed some twenty pounds and was a great deal like a dog, four-legged, a tail, long muzzle. It was gray like the frogs and had a ridge along its back.

The frogs sat beside it, talking to it and petting it, though the contact must have hurt their hands. It snorted and fought to catch its breath and by and by it lay quietly and didn't breathe much at all.

I felt bad even though it was the first time I had laid eyes on the creature. Some other frogs brought the body of another animal to the scene and laid it on the ground beside the old one. I knew the newcomer was dead for earlier I had seen it lying in the bushes on a slab of ice. It was of the same species as the old one but was much younger. At the time I had asked Felix what killed it and he said it drowned. That's why I knew it was dead when I saw it again.

The two animals lay side by side for a time, while a group of frogs knelt nearby and touched them both. The old one finally gave a slight gasp and all at once rolled over and died. At about the same time the young one snorted and raised its head. The next thing I knew it was walking around eating and carrying on as if nothing had happened to it.

I didn't understand what was going on. Maybe I had heard Felix wrong when he told me the pup drowned. It had looked dead when I saw it in the bushes but plainly it hadn't been because now it was full of pep and vinegar.

The frogs didn't seem to think anything was out of the ordinary, went back to their dinner and behaved as if it was just one of those things.

"Hold on for a second," I said to Felix. "What was that all about?"

"Not Earthly," he said, as if I didn't already know such was the case.

"What was it that you did?"

"Kanalba. Secret."

"Secret? Does that mean you can't tell me?"

"Kanalba. I could tell you but you still wouldn't know. It's a legend. A secret."

I didn't know what to think about that. He might mean I had to comprehend frog philosophy and culture in order to appreciate kanalba, or he might simply have no wish to explain it to me. I thought about it but I didn't forget it.

They finished eating; then about fifty of them tramped across the snow with me toward another Earth compound some five miles from the factory. It was a storage area where new machinery was kept. There were no guards because most of the equipment was bulky and too heavy to be carried away without a crane but there was a lock on the warehouse.

"We could have done this on our own," Felix said to me.

"Why didn't you?"

"We wanted to wait until one of you gave us permission."

The weak moonlight shone on all their faces as they gathered near the warehouse door. Their eyes were big and dark and seemed to glitter in the dimness. I still marveled that they had managed to stay alive in such a bleak atmosphere.

"This isn't exactly permission, you know," I said. "What I'm actually doing is helping you steal this engine."

Felix nodded his head, moved his feet up and down to improve circulation. "We understand. You're giving your sanction. Your friends won't like it. It's all right. We want to live."

"Did everybody wear boots like I advised so there won't be any bloody tracks leading away from here?"

"Yes, all. Tonight the wind and snow will cover our marks but we have boots like you said."

I yanked the lock off the door and opened it wide so they could all get inside. Since I didn't know an atomic engine from a dentist's chair they had to show me what they wanted. I had no idea how they knew, either. Probably kanalba.

There were three portables of different sizes on a platform at the far end of the place, three lead-colored humps that had never been used up here and likely never would be since those currently in operation scarcely ever broke down.

Around and around the three squat structures the frogs moved, probing, feeling, assessing, attempting to make a choice but having no wish to be hasty. I think they were feeling the machines with their minds, since they didn't know too much about mechanics. Later Felix told me that certain principles of physics were taught each new generation of frogs, just as legends on Earth were passed on to children, except in this case the frogs never changed the telling and never embellished the facts.

They finally chose the middle-size engine, indicating to me that they were ready. After looking at the thing I had my doubts because it was no two hundred pound can of garbage but weighed in the neighborhood of five tons. Sixteen feet high and twenty feet across, dark gray in color and scary looking when one considered its potential, the engine gave me the impression that it intended to sit where it was until doomsday. It would accept anything in its maw, from the proverbial soup to nuts, or from a chunk of rock to a cup of water, and it had the ability to blast atoms and create the heat of a tiny sun.

The frogs didn't seem awed but eager as they gathered around it in a tight circle and made lifting motions with their hands. Incredibly the thing groaned and moved up off the floor an inch or two. Half the group strained to keep it from falling while the other half climbed off the platform and directed the behemoth to come to them. It did. I found it hard to believe that a bunch of such little runts could make that metal monster behave like a human worker.

It came off the platform like a boat on an angry swell of ocean but then the frogs steadied it and directed it down the corridor between stacked equipment toward the door. Once they had the feel of it they could move fairly quickly and before I knew it the whole pack of them was out in the snow. The sad moon glinted off the engine and in a little while I couldn't see the frogs but only the big gray hump bouncing along toward the distant dunes.

I had Felix' assurance that they would install the thing in a most inhospitable spot so that humans wouldn't be overly persistent about finding it. He said it would be placed exactly where legend told them to apply heat if they ever had the opportunity, between the two largest oases on their world.

Installation would involve nothing more than finding a cavity in which to place the engine. Outside the warehouse, I stacked the tubing which would be picked up later by other frogs. It would be hooked to the engine's outlets, run into any areas they pleased and then the contraption would be ready to go. There was enough fuel in it to last several years. After that anything would do. There was nothing dangerous about using it out in the open as it had been built for just such use. The heat generated by the fission would convert the water fed into the maw into steam which led off through the tubes. That was all the frogs wanted, just the steam. They had no need of turbines to feed generators to make electricity. All they wanted was to melt ice.

I wondered if it would work and I had no idea what the frogs thought. It was the trying that counted. Scarcely anything in my life had ever really worked out but the attempts I made were important. Therefore I believed great strides had been made that night and after waving goodbye to the gray people I went home to bed.

Chapter 13

In the morning a new driver threw my roommates out of bed, literally. She was an air-headed novice whose thoughts were like chicken tracks, a mark here and a mark there with too much emptiness in between. I don't imply that she was stupid. A word that severe was reserved for people like me. Kalla was as intelligent as the next normal person. She was just a novice, but one Bates was tickled to death to get as it presented to her a possibility of getting rid of Peterkin.

Kalla hadn't come directly from Earth but from the domed colony that had been wasted by the deluge of oil. Instead of going back home with the other evicted experimenters, she requested temporary duty in the factory, though she hadn't expected to be trained as a driver. Still, she shrugged and took a stab at it. Like most people she wasn't very good at it at first. All her more primitive emotions came to the surface when she got her first close look at us; consequently everyone with the exception of myself made like a Keystone Kop.

"Another green driver," said Flora, picking herself up from the floor where she had fallen from the top bunk. Her false plate fell out and I made her stand still while I put it back in her mouth. She could have eaten without it and never known the difference but she might choke on something. Then the pack in her brain would probably blow a fuse in which case Zott, Frye and I would be due for a new roomie. I didn't want that to happen. I wanted all three of them to remain in good shape. Before we marched out that morning I checked each of them.

The hole in Frye's back, made by the hot cinder,

hadn't healed. It never would, but at least it wasn't rotting or getting bigger. I plastered it over with some flour I had stolen from the kitchen and then put a big Band-aid on it.

Zott was looking poorly these days. The circles around his eyes were the color of coal, which made me wonder if there was something wrong with his blood. Maybe the pack wasn't filtering it the way it should.

"Good looking, ain't I?" he said, grinning up at me. "At least I had that going for me when I was in the running."

"You sure are," I said, wondering how any woman ever could have found him attractive. Likely no one had. One thing I noticed in my celibate days on Earth was that too many men mistook the reasons why women were attracted to them. Most of the time it was money, security or prestige instead of love, desire or even affection.

"You sure are good-looking," I said, and shoved him out the door, where we fell in line with workers coming from other sections.

Kalla was young and pretty, dark of hair, and her almond-shaped eyes snapped with high spirit and energy. She was about the same size and shape as Bates.

She had us creaking and jerking up through the levels and along hallways until finally we reached the factory.

"I don't like her," said Zott. "She reminds me of my wife."

"She reminds me of òne of my kids," said Flora. "I like her."

"Me, too," said Frye. "She looks like my shrink."

Do this, do that, no excessive movements, quit jerking like Chaplin and get yourselves to your places of work. "How are you this morning?" Kalla said to us through the mike.

I wondered what she would have done had we returned her greeting. Fainted dead on the spot?

Do this, do that; occasionally she was apologetic when her nerves got in the way. Zottinger stumbled over a stray bar on the floor, causing her to scream at him but then she apologized in the next instant. Bates was up there in the booth giving her some pointers but I figured she must have been tutored for quite some time before being allowed to put on the hat.

"It's tough at first," said Bates. The mike was on so we all heard. "You'll be tempted to think of them as people. In fact they are people in that each of them has a kind of personality. Each has a unique way of walking and responding to orders. Some are slower than others but no one is fast."

"They're all pretty big, aren't they?" said Kalla. Her eyes were almost round as she stared down at us.

"They don't send us any weaklings."

"I thought it didn't make any difference what size they were. The packs keep them stimulated at top peak to make them abnormally strong."

"That's true," said Bates. "Still, it's more economical to send us specimens who are strong to begin with. That way even the roughest jobs aren't too much for them."

"Well, okay." Kalla nodded. "I think I can handle it."

"You'll have nightmares at first. Hang in there and you'll make it."

Bates went out to lunch and right away the young one started talking to us to steady her nerves. "I don't want to see anyone looking as if they're talking. That's forbidden. Drives me up the wall. Okay? Also, if you're doing your job and I leave you alone and direct my commands elsewhere, I don't want you gawking up here. It drives me crazy. Let's see, I guess what I really want you to do is behave like robots. No facial expressions, no reactions to anything but my orders, no unusual bodily movements. You know."

"They won't behave like robots," said Quidler, coming into the booth. His brown hair was plastered down and his homely face was sparkling clean.

"Why not?" said Kalla.

"Because they aren't machines. They get gas, indigestion, Charlie horses, bad backs and any number of afflictions. So how are you doing, toots?"

"That isn't my name and why are you in here?"

"See what I get for being polite? I could have totally ignored you and just gone down there and cut myself out a small posse. Special detail."

"Better not. Ignore me, I mean. I'm going to be your superior."

Quidler shook his head and grinned. "Pete's superior, maybe, but not mine. I have seniority over you. Bates is the only boss I got."

"Seniority is by job assignment, not time."

"Usually, yes, when the job is usual, which this one isn't. You didn't learn complicated things like that while you lived in the glass dome."

Kalla gave him a wry stare. "I can do without the condescension. As for the other, I'll check on it and if you're right I'll bow and scrape whenever I see you. In the meantime, you're interrupting me."

"I do that better than anything. If you don't believe me, ask Shirley." Quidler left the booth, came down the stairs into the work area and stood way over by the wall where it was relatively cool. Right away his eyes lit on me. Since I was standing up, I was very much unavoidable. He put on his little driver's hat and said, "You," three times, pointing.

The three of us were outfitted with coats and hats before we went out because we would be exposed to the cold for several hours and our skin might be damaged. Besides, Quidler wasn't as sadistic as Peterkin. Still, I didn't like him. He shoved me around as if I were a big stupid moron, and I wondered why he brought me along since the sight of me seemed to offend him so.

I soon ceased wondering when it became obvious my purpose in being there was to shove the sled out of deep gullies and up steep inclines when it bogged down. It was about fifteen feet long, a flat metal bed with rails for us workers to hold onto. The runners were strong and held us high off the ground. Quidler sat behind us on a comfortable seat housing the motor and told us what to do. While he remained on the sled, we trudged out into the wilds and signaled by raising our hands if we saw anything other than what he mentioned.

I saw to it that we didn't see anything. I knew Quidler had been sent to search for the missing atomic engine. Why else would anyone come out here? There was nothing for miles around but ice dunes, snow, fog, wind and desolation. Once we spotted an oasis but I wouldn't let the other two raise their hands when Quidler asked us if we saw any.

He ate sandwiches and I was glad he couldn't hear my stomach growl. So hungry was I that I was tempted to take the food from him and pitch him out into the snow but it was too far from home for him to make it back on foot. Besides, I didn't want to betray myself. Never again would I be a guinea pig for idiot scientists who had no respect for any kind of life.

Quidler spent the trip home cussing the planet and swearing at us for being so unreliable. "If I ever get out of this dump I never want to see another stiff as long as I live," he said aloud. "If anyone I know dies he'll have to have a funeral without me." Withdrawing into a brooding but brief silence, he stared bleakly out at the barren scene. He shivered and hunched his shoulders to get out of the wind. "Awful place," he muttered. "Land of the dead and the dying. Those frogs will never make it. Another century and they'll all be extinct."

He sounded sad but I don't think he was grieving over the planet's natives. It was himself for whom he felt sorry. Born a common sod, the only way he could climb the ladder was to put life and sanity on the limb.

Needless to say, we spotted no frogs with company property and finally headed toward home at sundown. The day had been long, dreary and uneventful. While we three workers fell into the end of the chow line, Quidler went off to tell Bates how he had wasted his time.

As I lay sleeping that night, someone came into the room. Whoever it was didn't turn on the light. Lying on my back, I suddenly opened my eyes as someone took hold of my hand. He was wearing gloves and it was all I could do to refrain from yanking him close to see who it was. He didn't do any more than that, simply took my hand in one of his and laid his other hand on my arm. He held me for a few moments and then let me go. I heard him walk out of the room and go down the hallway toward the stairs.

Meanwhile I lay wondering what he had thought he was up to. I didn't mind having been awakened since it was near the hour when it was time for me to take a bath. Once a week a driver herded the workers on our floor into a shallow tub in a stall at the end of the corridor. I never went with the others because I preferred doing my bathing alone and more often. Three nights a week I awakened early, took soap and towel, quietly entered the stall and walked into the pool which was always kept full of clean water. It didn't scare me or remind me of the lake back on Earth.

That night I did as before, waded in and gave myself a good scrubbing. At that hour no one was about. Because I wasn't fully alert, I washed away the green stains on my hand and arm without really noticing them. I'm sure they were there. Whoever had sneaked into my room intended to destroy me and my friends by leaving an infection on our skin.

Later I discovered it was a type of mossy fungus that attacked animal tissue with a virulence unknown practically anywhere else in the solar system. Indigenous to Land's End, it could be found only in the icy reaches where the dunes grew twenty and thirty feet high and where the wind howled like a gale. The fungus fed on the vegetation captured in the ice stalks, harmless-seeming because nobody had a use for it and left it alone. Except for whoever sneaked into my room that night and contaminated us.

In the morning it was Frye's and Flora's turn to get washed by me. Unfortunately for Zott, he carried his green stains about on him for several hours until it was too late. I didn't even notice them.

Having to live with the three, I made it as pleasant for

myself as possible by keeping them clean. A bath once a week was not enough, in my opinion. We worked hard, perspired freely, picked up all kinds of grit and grease from the factory and we got slopped on in the galley. I didn't care how often Bates ordered a change of clothes for all of us, which happened to be twice weekly. My roomies must be clean or I refused to sleep with them.

It hadn't seemed to matter how often LeMay bathed, but she was gone now so I tried to forget her. Flora would never take her place, but then no one could ever really substitute for another when it came to personality. Still, I tried to take care of the old woman, for my own sake, since it didn't matter to her one way or the other and hadn't mattered since the day she died. That she talked and frequently walked like my own little puppet was something I scarcely ever admitted to myself. To me she was real and in need.

"I'm never taking a bath with women," said Zott when the three of us came back from the washroom.

"You've done it before," said Frye. "In fact, you've done it plenty of times. In fact, how are you ever going to get washed around here unless you do it in the company of women? We outnumber you two to one."

"What, what?" he said, in obvious alarm. He looked at me. "Is it true? How can that be?"

"For some reason they send more women than men," I said. "I heard Kalla say more men die violent deaths than women and get their bodies all torn up. You can't use someone whose face has been shot to shreds or whose belly is ripped by a knife."

Zottinger was angry. "I've been hearing too much stuff like that. Too many statistics. Women this, women that. You'd think us guys were only kept around to maintain the herd."

"Some guys, maybe, but not you," said Frye. "You look like a monkey."

Zott stood there with the green stains on his arm and hand and I didn't really see them, particularly not as I waited for him to indulge in a fit of rage. Instead he sank down on his cot and stared up at us with sad eyes. "I know it," he said. "I was always an ugly little feller. Never could attract fancy women. I've had it in for the female of the species because my wife did me such dirt."

"You have a lot of nerve," said Flora. "It won't matter how much you badmouth her, you'll never come out looking clean. Wasn't it you took a gun and shot off the head of the gent who was courting her?"

"Nope."

The remark surprised us all. Flora cleared her throat and clicked her false teeth. "What's that you're saying? Are you adding a foul lie to the crime of murder?"

"Nope, because I never did it," said Zott. "She did it, not me. He was tired of her and intended to take off. She couldn't stand being humiliated and in a fit of passion plugged him. I took the rap and walked into the execution chamber with a lie on my lips. She didn't even come to see me while I was waiting to die. I've been bitter ever since. Can you blame me?"

Sooner or later we would have gotten around to discussing it except that we had to go to work and postponed the subject. A couple of days later an idiot in the cafeteria who was ladling out food onto our trays began yelling that Zott had a disgusting disease. It was a green growth on his cheek that attracted her attention. I had noticed it and it seemed to be fast-growing but I paid it little heed since I didn't know what it was. Once the stuff got a good hold in the tissues it was relentless, as I found out later.

The cook set to yipping and yapping and refused to serve anybody else and eventually a flunky came down to see what the fuss was about.

"That's nothing," he said in ignorance after inspecting Zott's green growth. "A little mold or something is all. What do you think this guy is, as fresh as an infant? Or maybe you think he's just a shell full of stuffing?"

"Don't go giving me any of your adolescent stupidity," snapped the cook. She looked a good deal like Mildred but was older and had more horsesense. "I've seen that disease before. If you don't get him away, he'll contaminate all the stiffs and then you'll have to do the factory work yourself. In fact you might catch it yourself."

Kalla was summoned but she didn't know what the thing on Zott's face was. Bates was hustled out of bed and brought on the double. She took one look at Zott, ordered him out of the line and marched away with him.

I found him late that night in the brig in the lower basement of our quarters. The ludicrous reality that the door was locked could be laid to the nervous and emotional state of the flunkies in charge. Somewhere along the line they began thinking of stiffs as spooks, and vice versa. Alone, Zott sat on a bunk in the dark staring at nothing. I gave him a biscuit and a pear and kept him company until the sun came up. Before I left I turned on the light to have a look at him. One whole side of his face was puffy and green.

The medics labored hard to save him because he was a valuable piece of property but the fungus raced ahead of them and ruined my poor friend. The last time I saw him his head looked like a large green hedgeapple with his facial features barely discernible.

I'm not sure what they did with him. I guess they most likely took him into the factory and had him climb into the vat. I don't know. I never saw him again.

I didn't stop wondering who it was that killed him. Whoever sneaked into our room that night infected us all with the disease. We women survived because we had a bath soon afterward. No, that wasn't exactly right. Flora hadn't had any green stains on her skin. I remembered how her arms looked in the light. Whoever had it in for us didn't care about Flora. They weren't trying to kill her, only the original quartet. Now LeMay and Zott were gone and just Frye and I were left.

Chapter 14

Peterkin complained that the basement was leaking. I didn't know what he meant. The building was made up of several levels and all were below ground except for the cafeteria and the galley, the factory and the top level. Besides, it was as cold as Billy Blue outside with everything hard and frozen, so how could anything be leaking through the walls?

Nevertheless a troop of us were made to tramp outside and dig about to see if there was a thawed area.

"This is dumb!" said the flunky who accompanied us. Peterkin stood in the galley doorway watching. "This is stupid!" the kid yelled. "It isn't even dawn, I haven't had breakfast and you've got us freezing our tails off for nothing! This whole planet has been frozen solid for a thousand years!"

"It's leaking in your own quarters downstairs!" Peterkin yelled back. "Don't you care?"

"No!" Glancing at me, the kid said, "He's done this before, you know. I think he's nuts. You can bet on it, there's no point in our being out here except for his ulterior motives."

I didn't say anything back since I had no wish to further erode his already fragile equilibrium. Besides, he wasn't the kind of person I would talk to, anyway.

We walked all around the building, poking in the snow for soft spots or weak places, and by and by I noticed that Peterkin was breaking us up into groups. I don't know if he expected us to act like the flunky and run to him everytime we had something to comment about. No, of course he didn't. Maybe the metal sticks we poked up and down in the snow gave off signals when they rammed into something soft. Maybe that was it. For some reason the whole business didn't seem to make any sense. I and two other workers were getting farther and farther from the others and once or twice we went around a corner out of sight.

The two bruisers with me kept looking at me and crowding me. I heard the flunky yelling and then he came around the corner to glare at us.

"How come these three are over here by themselves?" he bellowed.

"Mind your own business!" said Peterkin, coming to the corner to look at us. "Instead of getting in my hair why don't you take your stupid stick and get the devil around the other end of the building?"

Muttering to himself, the kid went away and left us but I could still hear him griping long after I lost sight of him.

In a little while my two companions stopped doing anything at all and simply stood in the snow staring at nothing. Since Peterkin was telling me through my pack to do the same thing, I stopped poking with my stick and waited to see what was going to happen.

The world was cold and quiet, darkly gray and alien in a way it had never seemed to me before. There might not have been another living soul standing and blowing white puffs into the air. My two companions did likewise but only because machinery forced them to do so. Ignoring the manipulative touches inside my head, I did as I pleased, wandered about, stared up at the sky and speculated as to why loneliness always felt the same no matter where I was.

At about that time one of my associates came up to me and swung his stick at my head with the intention of knocking my brains out. He missed because his coordination was naturally poor and the heavy rod came down on the fleshy part of my shoulder. I wasn't certain whether or not my collarbone broke. It felt like a mountain dropping on me and I grunted and went down on one knee. That saved me from being brained by the second stiff whose stick whistled over my head and hit the other guy in the side.

It took me some agonizing moments to get the picture clear in my mind. That's the way I was. Slow and confused. The stiffs were only supposed to obey Peterkin's commands because he wore the driver's hat but he was way around the other side of the building manipulating the others. I didn't think he could direct these two so expertly without being able to see them. Besides, why would he tell them to break my bones?

I was like that, slow to move because I was a slow thinker, and I was even slower when I couldn't understand any part of what was happening. The two guys weren't behaving like stiffs but seemed to be primed solely to bash me into an inanimate hulk, which I later decided was the case. Their packs had been fiddled with. It was possible for a person who was clever with miniature electronics to diddle with the visible wiring on a stiff's neck and have his way with it. These two men in the darkness and the cold had been given a prime directive similar to a robot command. Their wiring was tied off so that the one command echoed and reechoed in their heads without altering or ceasing. Their job was to kill me.

Kill a worker? No one knew I was alive. Probably the directive was to render me inoperable or useless. One of them carried a butcher knife in his back pocket, no doubt meaning to fix me so that I couldn't walk anymore.

One took me by the throat while the other raised his stick high. It hit me on the tip of my elbow as I moved aside. Since that arm was numb, I used my other to shove the strangler back onto the snow. Number two made like a baseball slugger with the stick and caught me across the thigh.

I looked around to see if anyone else was near but it was all right. We three were all alone waging a senseless battle. I guess death wasn't enough for Peterkin. What did you call killing a dead person? What did he call it? For some reason I was a threat to him, just as LeMay and

Zott had been threats. A couple of inexplicable things had happened to him while he was with us so he decided to get rid of his confusion and bewilderment in a manner that came naturally to him: get rid of the confusing item or items.

The clobbering of my elbow made me mad, likewise the stupid persistence of my assailants angered me. I didn't like being stuck up here on a no-man's land, didn't like never having been asked if I wanted to go into space, hated the idea that I was despised by Peterkin enough for him to want to destroy me. Then too, I didn't enjoy ruining a couple of perfectly good workers.

They wouldn't respond to my mental commands. I tried that first of all but Peterkin had been thorough when he jammed their circuits. Their sole delight was to see me pulverized into the snow and they did their very best to obey orders.

I didn't want to do it but it had to be done. Besides, I was mad. Grabbing the stick from number two, I swung it through the air at the strangler who was just then getting to his knees. It broke his neck, not just a little but all the way so that his head hung down his back like the hood on a sweater. Since his view of things became lopsided he couldn't find me to wreak damage upon me. He started walking around in circles and the last I saw of him he was trying to climb the side of the building.

What I did to the remaining one wasn't a good thing to do but I had no choice. Knowing perfectly well he was or had once been someone's father or brother, I grabbed him as he rushed me, picked him up with no effort and slammed him hard across my knee. His back snapped like kindling so that when I dropped him he lay still like the corpse he had been all along. No matter how many packs he had in his head, forever after today he would be motionless. No electronic signals would ever again travel through his shattered body.

Sore of shoulder and heart, I stumbled around the building and joined the others as they filed inside. Peterkin was no longer there but only the flunky was present to drive us. As the warmth of the galley flooded over me, I hoped Peterkin slept well that night. I more or less intended it to be his last peaceful one.

It turned out that it wasn't. Peaceful, I mean, but at the time I had no inkling of his plan. In the wee hours of the morning I walked into the tub in the basement, soaked in hot water and tried to get the pain out of my shoulder and thigh. The former didn't seem to be broken but every time I moved my arm it felt as if every tendon I owned started yelling. There was a fat red welt across my thigh. Other than that, the intended murder victim was in good shape.

I didn't see Peterkin all that day, so I assumed he believed I was finished. Sometime during the afternoon the two dead corpses were found in the snow and speculation was rampant as to what happened to them.

Not too hungry at dinnertime, I realized in the middle of the night that I was starving so I dressed and ascended a few flights to the cafeteria. I didn't go straight up because something happened on the third level that caused me to hesitate and even go down a hallway to investigate.

As I rounded the stairs and had my hand on the newel post to continue my climb to the fourth floor, I heard what sounded like a muffled scream. Slowly I turned my head and stared down the dim corridor. It looked empty and I was in the act of turning away when there came the sounds of a groan followed by a thud.

Without a sound I started down the hall. At the far end, a bedroom door opened and someone came out. She didn't glance back my way but slowly walked toward another figure standing in the shadows. Together they pushed through the swinging doors and disappeared.

I wish I had gone after them and caught them then. I would have nabbed a killer, saved lives and spared myself a lot of suffering.

There were no more noises then so, after standing and peering at shadows for several minutes, I shrugged and went on up to the cafeteria. For a change, Mildred wasn't there. It could be that she was tired, or it could be some ray of intelligence finally filtered into her consciousness to tell her I wasn't really like the other workers. Was the truth more than she cared to face? Did she wonder what it was like to live with the dead, to be considered no more than a soulless sod, to be alive and in hell? Did she or anyone have that much imagination?

I ate my fill and went back to bed. Lying there in the blackness staring up at nothing, I got to thinking about the two people I had seen in the hallway. It made me uneasy to admit both had seemed familiar to me.

On impulse I bounded out of bed, turned on the light and went over to look at my friends. Flora was all right, lay on the other top bunk with her eyes closed like a good little worker. Then I checked Frye beneath her. Frye's eyes were closed but there wasn't much else about her that was ordinary. She was covered with blood and lying across her body was a spattered axe.

It took me a minute to realize she wasn't cut or damaged in any way. Quickly I stripped off my clothes, picked up the axe and laid it on the bundle so no stains would mar the floor. I don't know how she had gotten into bed without dripping but no matter how carefully I scrutinized the floor, furniture and hallway, I could find no blood.

"Get up, Frye," I said to her and she opened her eyes. "Get up," I said again.

Obediently she arose, stripped and followed me out of the room and down the hall to the tub. I scrubbed her from head to toe with strong soap, scrubbed myself, rinsed us both and then drained the tub and refilled it.

After I dried us off, we went back into our room and my companion stood to one side while I made her bed. Quietly she got between the fresh sheets, shut her eyes and went limp.

Wrapping the stained sheets and clothing around the axe, I sneaked upstairs and went outside where I buried it all in the snow.

Long afterward I lay in my bunk and tried to sleep but it didn't work. In my mind I kept seeing Frye coming out of that bedroom on the third floor.

Toward morning a pair of flunkies came in and turned on the light. They walked over to the beds and looked us over. "I don't know why we had to come in here and check these stiffs," said one. "Do you suppose it's some kind of practical joke?"

"Beats me," said the second boy, his voice thick with weariness. "Well, we did like we were told. We came in, we turned on the light and we looked around."

"So we did and it was a blasted waste of time."

As they both started out, the first one said, "I'm going to complain about this. Who gave the dumb order for us to come in here?"

"I don't know. It sounded over the squawk box and you know how that thing fractures sound. Forget it. Let's go back to bed."

Chapter 15

Being more intelligent was no fun. It was easier to be a dimwit. I suppose the pack in my head coordinated my thought processes with more facility than nature had condescended to do. Not that I was a genius and not that I was better equipped to handle my problems. There were serious lapses in my logic and memory, while half the time I didn't even recognize problems until they exploded over my head.

I could scarcely recall the institution where I had spent most of my life. That might have been because I actively disliked it or it could be that the boredom of it all drove it straight out of my recall.

I used to find it strange that no one on Land's End, with the exception of Mildred, noticed that I was different from the other workers, but then there was the fact that people didn't really look at any of us. They utilized peripheral vision when in our presence or they caused a glaze to come over their eyes, or they pretended that their sight was blurred whenever they were near us. All did that except Peterkin, who began watching me like a hawk after he saw me again and realized I was still going strong. I don't think he ever faced the fact that I was a living woman and it wasn't just because I was so hard to look at. He was insane and had been that way long before he was shipped to Land's End to become one of the staff. In his mind it was better to work here than rot in an Earth jail.

I missed LeMay and Zott. So apparently did my alter-consciousnesses or whatever part of me it was that presumed or assumed identities in my roommates.

"I want to die," said Frye. "Why did Zott and LeMay have to go away? Every time I find a friend something happens to them."

"At least you have your memories," I pointed out to her.

"Big deal. It's like I'm haunted by visions of myself trying to kill my kid."

"What happened to her?"

"I don't know, fortunately. I don't even know what happened to me."

"You killed yourself, or have you forgotten? You cut your wrists."

With a wave of her hand, she said, "I was always doing stuff like that but it never worked. Once I swallowed thirty sleeping pills and they didn't kill me."

"I expect the doctors pumped out your stomach."

"What doctors? I never saw a doctor. I was holed up in a fleabag all by myself, no pals around except for two or three cockroaches. It was a Friday afternoon when all those little naps went down my hatch. The following Thursday I woke up bombed out of my mind."

Shaking my head, I said, "We've got housekeeping duty today. Let's get dressed."

Reluctantly she climbed out of bed. "Why do they make us wear clothes? What do they care?"

"They don't want to be looking at a bunch of bare behinds. It would make us seem more alive and that would give them extra nightmares. Also, clothes protect our skin."

We made beds and scrubbed floors on the third level while Quidler drove us and sneaked sucks from a brown bottle. I wasn't sure but I suspected that everyone alive and over twenty five on Land's End was a drunk.

"You're the biggest dame I ever saw in my life," he said to my back. He was nearly to the hiccup stage. "You were a body builder, I'll bet good money. What happened? Did you drop one of your weights on your head?"

I ignored him and swabbed the floor.

"Put down the mop and see if you can lift that stove," he said.

Dropping my tool with a clatter, I headed for the potbelly in the corner. Doubt and confusion rising in my thoughts, I walked slowly, in no hurry to reach my destination. Did Quidler have it in his head to burn my arms off and render me unfit for work? That stove was filled to the brim with coal and was the color of a rose.

Just before I reached it he said casually, "Not that one, dummy. The other one. The cold one."

The pipe had broken on the second stove and it sat in the corner like a burnt and blackened beetle. A big bruiser, it must have weighed six hundred pounds, but I could have lifted the whole thing had there been convenient hand grips. As it was, I hauled most of it off the floor and showed Quidler more than he bargained for.

Turning a little green and losing his appetite for booze, he quietly ordered me to set the thing back down and to quit tearing up the floor.

"Holy rotgut!" he whined over and over again. "Did you ever! My aching kidneys! Hey, you, pick up your mop and swab the joint, eh, and I'll pretend I didn't see what I just saw. It didn't happen anyway."

He didn't want anything more out of the ordinary in his life. Enough was already enough.

"Hey, you, just because your hair is gray doesn't mean you can goldbrick!" he yelled at Flora. "Not around here you can't! Tote that water bucket! Lift that mop! Dunderheads! Cryptmeat!"

He didn't really look at us. Glimpses of a bit of dingy skin, a tattered cuff, a hank of hair were sufficient for him to know where we were. He was already rightly aware of what we were. The walking dead. Mobile stiffs. Cheap labor. Obedient slaves. Coffin sand. Do this, do that, and never mind what you used to be in living reality. This, my friend, is limbo and if the ghosts of your past yet prowl and screech inside your psyche, that's too bad for you.

The day rolled on while we did our work without complaining, and I don't know what time it was when a flunky came in to tell Quidler about Kalla. It hit him like a ton of bricks because—well, I'm not sure, it might have been a guilty conscience, though his wasn't noisily active. Not moribund, just feeble.

While I worked I listened to the conversation and what I heard made me sweat. Kalla had been found dead in her room on the third floor. During the night somebody had killed her.

Green of face, hiccupping, walking more like a stiff than a stiff, Quidler up and left us flat as he walked out of the room. The flunky went with him which meant there was no driver so everyone prepared to fall flat on their faces. I didn't let them do that, handled them with no trouble and had them find a clean place on a bunk to sit down.

We waited and waited but nobody came back to tend us so I ordered everyone to lie down on the bunks and close their eyes. Then I went out. Later a couple of flunkies came into the room and saw the arrangement I had made. After their initial reaction they went to Bates and applied for transfers back to Earth.

Meantime I went to the third floor to see if I could acquire some more information. I had heard Kalla being killed. I knew I had, and I'd seen Frye and her murderer leave the room and escape through the swinging doors. The knowledge that my senses hadn't been keen enough to cause me to investigate the cries I heard filled me with anger and grief. Poor little Kalla, tough and gritty, wanting to become an expert driver like Bates. Why did she die? Because she was good at her work? Or because she was pretty? Or both?

The hallways were clogged with staff members and a few workers on errands for specific individuals. I was spotted right away but no one took unusual notice of me, naturally assuming that I was being driven by someone.

The area outside Kalla's room was too jammed for me to get near it so I stood at an intersection and looked over the heads of those around me. I saw Bates and a few flunkies I knew by sight. Quidler was there but I wasn't interested in any of them. I was looking for Peterkin and then I saw him standing against the wall with his eyes shut. He looked peculiar with his back rigidly against the wall that way, as if he were being stalked by something frightening, but everyone was too busy asking questions and dealing with their own emotions to notice him. They didn't know or care that at least momentarily something was very wrong with Peterkin.

He saw me first. His eyes flicked open as if his subconscious had sounded a warning and the very first object his mind grabbed was me. There I was sticking up in the crowd like a treetop and the savagery that leaped into his expression caused the hair on the back of my neck to stir.

He wasn't looking at a worker or a living person or anyone at all, but merely at something he hated. Neither he nor I knew why he suddenly began loathing me so much. It was my opinion that he sensed my original attraction to him when I came to Land's End and his subconscious was so outraged and offended that he reacted by wanting to kill me. That was pretty much the way a maniac responded to things. With blind fury. With persistently negative emotion. Peterkin didn't know what or why I was but he wanted to put a stop to my existence on every plane.

Over the crowd I watched him and tried reading his thoughts. That he wasn't done with me was evident to see in his expression. I only wondered what his next move would be. Plainly it wasn't going to be then and there because the look on his face suddenly became bland and empty.

Later in our room I had private words with Frye. "I'm wondering if I can get some information from you about last night?"

"Personally I think it's hopeless," she said. "As far as I'm concerned you're only talking to yourself." She didn't look well today but it had little to do with her activities. Mostly it had to do with how well the pack in her head carried out its function of keeping her bodily processes regular. Sometimes it faltered and a little corruption crept in.

"Let's both pretend I'm not talking to myself. Besides, they didn't allow your brain cells to destruct before they implanted that pack. Some of them had to be alive, otherwise you'd be moldering in a grave on Earth."

"True, but you want to know about last night and that's a new experience. My brain doesn't grow new cells. In fact it's in the same condition it was in when they plugged my skull with the pack. No cell division, no growth and a little rot that seems unavoidable."

"Don't be smart," I said. "Not that way, anyhow. Where were you last night?"

"In bed. Where else?"

"You were in Kalla's room last night. You killed her with an axe."

All of a sudden she sat down hard on her bunk. "Are you telling me I killed my kid?"

"No, no, get your head together. I'm not talking about your daughter. I'm talking about Kalla."

She held up her hands and stared at them. "They told me she was fine. They told me she married some nice boy and moved away."

The way she looked and what she said upset me. Maybe I supplied most of the energy but her locked brain cells weren't as inert as I might have wished. Like a classic case of regression, she straddled a single period in her past and refused to budge.

"Who was in the hall with you last night?" I said. "Who ordered you to do what you did?"

"I was in bed last night. I didn't do anything."

"Where did you get the axe?"

"From the garage, where else? My husband bought it just before he walked out on me. I didn't kill her. I came out of my psychosis and stopped trying to get into her room."

"You're talking too loudly. Lower your voice."

Staring up at me with glittering eyes, she said, "You're getting on my nerves. If I had an axe right now I'd use it on your head."

So much for a friendly conversation.

Kalla's killer was trying to cover his tracks. The two flunkies had been ordered to come into my room to look around because they were supposed to have discovered Frye lying in the dead woman's blood with the axe to hand. A furor would have ensued, Frye would have been examined and speculation would be excessive. Probably the final opinion would have been that something went wrong with Frye's pack that caused her to go berserk. They would wonder where she got the axe since there were none in her sleeping quarters or in her work areas. They would wonder about a lot of things but after she was deactivated and dumped in the vat all the questions would be forgotten. Both Kalla and Frye would have been disposed of.

That wasn't the way it was going to be, though. My roommate wasn't implicated in Kalla's murder. None of the workers were. Bates and the authorities would be going on the hunt for a living killer.

Chapter 16

The day we cleaned the library I found out a few things about Peterkin. The two flunkies driving us were slothful and took an extra long lunch break so that I was able to use the computer. To get to the machine I had to pull a couple of workers out of the way. The flunkies had done what they were expressly forbidden to do, removed their hats before leaving and watched everybody fall down. Filled with disgust, I merely sat in a chair until they got all the giggling out of their systems and went away to the cafeteria.

In a way the room was forbidding, what with the many book shelves and the reading and taping machines. There were no patrons in the place since it was closed for cleaning.

A tape alone wouldn't have done me any good because I didn't know how to read so I approached the voice computer and told it to give me a report on Peterkin. Then I stood where I was and listened.

He had a wife and children on Earth that he hadn't seen in a long time, not that it probably mattered much to him since he ran out on them. It seemed that Land's End was the end of the line for him. He either made good here or it was a lifetime in San Quentin for him. Gambler, second-story expert, scammer, lecher and blackmailer, so much for a man who looked like a grown-up choir boy, and it went a long way toward proving that looks weren't proof of much of anything. No wonder Bates had been trying to get rid of him. In fact she had undoubtedly raised noisy objections when she found out he was coming from Earth. An habitual criminal, he had been diagnosed as a sociopath by a list of psychiatrists that read like Who's Who in brainwork, had spent a third of his life in jail and was threatened with more if he got into trouble.

Maybe they thought back there that he couldn't do much damage driving a bunch of stiffs. I don't know. I guess they were trying to do a human salvage job and couldn't distinguish between useable material and garbage, not that it was such a big oversight on their part. I hadn't been able to make the distinction either.

I sat back down in the chair in the library and gazed at all the books on the shelves around and above me. It seemed to me that they were a monumental amount of subjective opinion. One man's meat was another man's poison, one man's fact was another's fancy. Viewed by the bitter eye of infallibility, the sum total of our tomes must have seemed like so much caterwauling. Certainly mine wasn't that perfect eye. I had never even had a conversation with an intelligent person, though I had listened in on sufficient talks to lead me to believe people were so busy trying to construct mental highways and tributaries that they lost sight of their premises or the need for same.

Later on in the week, some high-paid people came in to conduct an investigation regarding the murder. They walked about looking important, but they also looked upset whenever they saw a worker. It was the first time for them. They were from another planet in the solar system and since Land's End was the only world where workers were employed, the bigwigs were naturally distressed by us.

I heard one of them talking to Bates in the glass booth in the factory and I could understand why she was relieved when he left.

"I want to help you all I can in the investigation," she said. "I think the first thing you ought to do is question the staff. Naturally I've already talked to most of them."

"The first thing we have to do is requisition some decent boots," said her visitor. He was a twerp named

Sanderson and it seemed to make him aggressive that everyone down in the work area was larger than he.

Having had plenty of experience with dunderheads, Bates was polite. "I beg your pardon?"

"I mean I nearly drowned trying to get into the blasted building! Don't you have any influence over the immediate surroundings?"

"Are you asking me if I can control the weather?"

Sanderson was snappish. "That isn't what I'm talking about. The pathways around the buildings are sopping wet. I should think for the sake of convenience you would do something about the water."

"There's a lot of melting of the ice in the vicinity. I intended trying to find the cause and a remedy when the killing took place. The murder. Miss Wru. Kalla Wru."

"How can I forget her? I want you to know we don't like it, nor do the company leaders like it."

"I don't like it, either," said Bates, her voice calm. "I didn't like it when you sent me a psychotic convict and I didn't like it when you ignored my requests to get rid of him."

"You've no proof Peterkin did it."

"Of course he did it. Kalla was his replacement. Maybe I couldn't have gotten him sent home but I surely would have gotten him out of my command. Evidently the idea displeased him."

Maybe Sanderson didn't feel spiteful but he looked it when he smiled. "You think the man couldn't bear the thought of being transferred so he up and chopped a girl to death, thereby earning himself a terminal hypo?"

"I don't really know why he did it. Why don't you ask him?"

Sanderson's finger came up to point at her throat. "Mind you, I intend to see justice done here, and fast, but I have to do it my way, if it's all right with you."

"It is. It's just that since I've been here a while and am familiar with the atmosphere I think my recommendations ought to be worth something."

"Ordinarily they would be, but this is a criminal situation and out of your experience. I'll find out who did it but it has to be my way."

"That makes sense. Why don't you go do it and stop worrying about getting your feet wet?"

She shouldn't have said it. Sanderson wasn't all that bad but he was tired and henpecked by his superiors so whenever an opportunity to step on an underling came his way he just naturally had to grab it. With his chin held high and his face the color of paper, he almost literally dragged his feet as he left the booth, and definitely he dragged them ever after.

Peterkin wasn't locked up or even questioned, as far as I knew. Of course there weren't too many people I could ask. I was tempted to inquire of Mildred that night when I went snack-hunting, but what with the killing of Kalla she was much too close to the point of no return. Her exhausted mien, her unkempt, stringy hair and her burning eyes staring at me as I ate a ham sandwich warned me to lay off and utter not a peep.

As for my roommates, they weren't exactly fonts of information but they could be other things now and then. Menacing, for instance. With the ham sandwich gurgling in my stomach, I fell asleep only to awaken in the dead of night to discover them both standing beside my bunk with weapons in their grasp. Flora held a butcher knife while Frye had hold of a long and wicked-looking axe. Not the one I buried in the snow. Peterkin had provided her with a new one.

"Back off," I said to them, hoping he hadn't messed with their wires the way he had with the two men he sent after me. I liked these women, particularly Frye, and had no wish to kill them. Ruin them. Sometimes it was confusing.

Flora obeyed at once, lowered the knife and tossed it in a corner.

"Well?" I said to Frye.

She looked like warm death standing there with her eyes big and shiny and her face as sallow as wax. Shoving her aside, I hopped from the bunk and hurried out into the hall. It was empty. No one was there. He was clever, wasn't he? Peterkin knew how to give a worker a delayed command.

I put the knife and axe under the spare mattress and then tied Frye and Flora to their beds. Still, it wasn't enough and I couldn't fall asleep again. Wide of eye, I lay brooding until Bates' cheerful call from the factory sounded in my head in the morning. Untying my companions, I trooped out in the hall with them and upstairs to work. For a change I looked every bit as bad as everybody else, slump-shouldered, exhausted, hollow of eye, dead, really.

After dinner that night ten of us were assigned to galley duty with Quidler pulling the puppet strings. He didn't look so hot these days, either, what with his haunted expression, lack of appetite and eye tics. I didn't blame him for being nervous.

He got mad because the frogs sneaked in out of the cold and sat on the floor beside the warm tins of garbage. "It's all your fault!" he yelled at them, standing with his arms akimbo and his legs spread. Obviously he knew how foolishly he behaved because there were two bright spots of embarrassment on his cheeks. It was only natural for him to let off steam at someone and he chose the little gray aborigines because they responded to rage more readily than we workers. "You're responsible for our troubles, you mangy little beggars!" he said. "Whose fault is it that you can't survive on your own world? Is it mine? You're getting your revenge by setting something loose in the air. A voodoo miasma or something!"

The frogs had gotten to their feet and were waiting to see if he was going to grow angry enough to chase them. I came up behind him and tipped over a tub of salad on his head. He let out a squawk and whirled on me. Like a good worker, I stood still while he identified and consigned to Hades me and my sub-human ancestors.

"If I didn't know better I'd think you did that on purpose!" he said, picking carrot strips from his hair. "This dump isn't fit for pigs to work in!" He threw a scrap of lettuce in my face but I didn't flinch. "Don't move!" he said. "Stand right there until your ugly bones rot!" Turning back to the frogs, he continued his emotional tirade. "This bloody planet ought to be stuffed with anti-matter. I say blow it to the devil and all you beggars along with it! The stinking place is melting water all over and I haven't got a pair of decent boots! How am I supposed to do a day's work when I'm surrounded by hideous corpses and a pack of sniveling little creeps?"

I upended a tub of rinse water on his head. It hit him hard enough to knock him onto his belly on the pile of salad. He screamed and tried to get to his feet but as he did so his hat fell off and a worker toppled onto him. Another knocked over a precariously-balanced can of soup. The frogs quickly levitated a full tub of meat and mixed vegetables and walked out the door with it. By the time Quidler got to his knees and looked behind him to see if I was for real, I was seated on the floor looking mindless.

He didn't get all the way up and in fact leaned against a table leg and groaned. It was all too much for him. Disobedience, murder, fear, nothing stable or static in his life—it was more than he could handle. Leaning back, he closed his eyes and sniffled.

Chapter 17

"It is kanalba," Felix said to me and then wouldn't elaborate. He needn't have, anyway, for I had learned enough to know that kanalba meant nature. Doing what came naturally. If the ice was melting, it was only because it was a natural consequence. But after such a long time and so suddenly?

"Kanalba," he said.

"Are you happy about it?" I said.

"Sure."

"Are you sad about it?"

"Sure."

"What does that mean?"

"Kanalba is all things and all feelings. I'm glad it worked."

"What worked?" I said.

"The atomic engine."

I felt a stirring in the bottom of my stomach. I had wanted to help him and his people but had I planned to go this far?

Because I was persistent he explained to me about the chemistry of heat and cold. It was all relative, he said. Then he talked about big dunes being little molecules of frozen water all stuck together. If one could alter the structure of one molecule, perhaps the entire dune could be affected.

Between the two largest oases on Land's End, approximately fifty miles away from my compound, was a buried volcano; a very big one. Legend had it that if the ice cap in the volcano crater melted, Land's End would revert to her natural state. Which was? Kanalba. Why ask Felix? He had only been around sixty years or so and hadn't the faintest idea.

They liked our garbage. Soup, salad, meat, bread, anything they could get their little teeth into they devoured, but they scarcely grew at all. Their young ones seemed to stay little for the longest time before their bodies lengthened. I think it meant they had a long life span. When I wasn't busy worrying about things, I pitied the frogs because they were like humans and pretended their lives were in order while their surroundings tumbled down.

Sanderson made no headway in his investigation, if indeed that was what he conducted. He wiped his balding head a great deal, inspected his wet shoes and cuffs, kept his eyes off the workers and strode about as if he had important destinations. It was obvious that he hadn't. Once I overheard him and one of his agents discussing the weather and it occurred to me that possibly he hadn't been sent to Land's End to solve Kalla's murder at all but to get to the bottom of the mystery of the melting ice. In both instances I was wrong. Sanderson had been sent to check on a private experiment the company conducted upon Peterkin, but I didn't find that out until later. It didn't matter anyhow since Sanderson didn't know enough about people to make sound judgments. He was too easily offended by unusual happenings to be effective on an alien world. Why he didn't just tell Bates what his mission really was instead of subjecting himself and his companions to her harping I couldn't say.

I visited the library late one night, made a tape recording in my own voice and laid it on Bates' desk in the factory booth so that she discovered it that afternoon when we workers filed into the factory. During the morning we had bagged sawdust and laid the bags against the outside of the building.

As soon as Bates found the tape she called Sanderson who came when he was summoned but made no secret of the fact that he didn't like it. He had a cold and his sniffles were picked up on the microphone and broadcast down in the work area.

"I don't suppose you know anything about this," she said, holding up the tape.

"How could I? What is it?"

"It was left here in a secretive fashion for me to find when I came in. I played it because I thought it might be instructions from you."

Sniffling and stamping his sodden feet, Sanderson peered closely at her to make certain there was no levity or sarcasm in her expression. "That's not a bad idea, except that it isn't the case. I didn't leave it and as far as I know none of my associates would do such a thing."

She played the tape and they both listened.

"Dear Bates,
This planet is going to drown. That is

my opinion. The frogs used an atomic engine to melt a big volcanic cap. I think you
should get everybody out of here before
things really begin to float.

                      A friend."

Sanderson heard it to the end before he began
snirkling. "A practical joke! Idiocy! Imagine one little engine warming up an entire world. The conditions in this
frozen dump haven't altered an iota for millennia."

Bates wasn't as casual about it. Her expression a com-
bination of doubt and unease, she locked the clip on the
tape and put it in her pocket. "Is it possible that this is a
ploy of Peterkin's to muddle the issues?"

"Hardly," Sanderson said in a dry voice. "Have you
checked his I.Q? Whoever made that tape can't be very
bright."

"Why not?"

"I've already told you. No amount of atomic engines
can melt a world caught in the grip of an ice age."

"Is that so? Maybe you can explain the presence of all
those warm oases. I've always wondered about them."

Blowing his nose, Sanderson said, "Have you ever
heard of desert oases?"

"Is that really relevant? I want to know how there can
be warm havens in the middle of a glacier. It seens to
me—"

"I can see you're no geologist."

"No, I'm not, but for a while I've been wishing I had
one here."

I think Sanderson was dying to tell her he was one, but
then if he did she might demand proof and he would be
forced to back down. If he had any real skills none of us
ever saw them. It only proved that Company Headquarters was no more efficient than anybody. They sent a
middleman who had about as much finesse as an ava-
lanche. My opinion was that no matter what he attempted
to do he wouldn't do it well. He was too worried about
one-upmanship and wet feet.

"Let me have that tape," he said to Bates.

"I'd rather keep it."

"I insist. I'll find out who is responsible for it and personally interrogate them."

Bates handed the thing over and Sanderson went away with it, muttering to himself about insurbordinates and high water. He hadn't a hope of tying the tape to me because he didn't know I existed. We workers were anathema to him and he ignored us as studiously as an alcoholic ignored hallucinations.

The walls of the lowest basement began leaking, so instead of sleeping that night we workers were called from our beds to move everything essential to the next highest level. I was sorry to see the place flooding because it meant I got no more hot baths. Worse, my roommates would get no more.

Beds, washing machines, the personal belongings of the flunkies quartered farther down the hall, linen supplies and several other items were trundled upstairs and made room for wherever it could be found.

I was quartered in an open dorm with ten other workers. Frye and Flora were there with me. After the flunkies no longer required our strong backs, they had us lie on our bunks and then they removed their drivers' hats and went away. Their own beds were in the middle of the hallway, mere yards away. They closed our door firmly, as if that placed extra distance between us.

Once everything quieted down and order was restored and the lights were extinguished, I headed down to the next level to see how the leaking was proceeding. As I passed by some flunkies bedded down in the corridor, one of them raised up and nudged a nearby companion.

"Am I seeing things? Isn't that one of those stiffs?"

"Don't be stupid. Of course it isn't."

"Hey, listen, we don't have any women that big. Or men, either, for that matter."

"Pipe down, will you? I've had a hard day. If the stiffs want to walk around, let them. I'm too tired to care."

The first one didn't get up and turn on the light. I expect he disliked the thought of what he might see. He settled down to some quiet complaining while I continued to the end of the corridor and descended the stairs.

It was worse than I expected. In fact it had to be worse than anyone anticipated. Instead of finding a couple of inches of water on the floor there was at least a foot of the stuff. The trickles and spurts that prompted Bates to evacuate the level had graduated to steady streams that found entrance through every crack in the walls. The bags of sawdust we had stacked against the building did no good at all.

By morning there were two feet of water down there but I was the only one who knew about it. The flunkies were always too lazy to do anything they weren't ordered to do so we all trooped to our respective duty stations while a little bit of Land's End seeped inside our home.

"I had the lower level evacuated because of the tape someone left on my desk," Bates said. She was in the glass booth talking to Quidler and Peterkin. A couple of times she told Peterkin to leave but he didn't, dawdled about her office touching things. Now he turned to her and laughed.

"You're superstitious," he said. "Someone leaves a dumb recording telling you the place is melting and you believe it."

Looking at Quidler, Bates said, "Why isn't he in the brig? My orders were—"

"Have you forgotten the brig is flooded? Besides, Sanderson ordered him freed."

"He's a nice fellow," Peterkin said idly, looking at neither of them. "He has a rational head on his shoulders."

"Since you're free for duty why don't you go and do some?" said Bates. "The sawdust baggers need a driver. I guess you can do that."

Peterkin looked at her with a little smile. "Sure," he said. "Okay." He went out and down the stairs toward the cafeteria which was nowhere near the north wing where the baggers labored.

As soon as he was gone, Bates turned on Quidler. "Are you crazy?"

"I didn't do it!"

"Turning him loose like that! Are you nuts?"

"The blasted brig is flooded and after I locked him in the library Sanderson let him out. He said the company doesn't want any lawyer claiming an innocent man was persecuted."

"Innocent, my eye!" Reaching out, Bates tapped him on the chest. "Listen to me and I don't want you to miss anything. I'm in charge here, do you get that? Well, do you?"

"I get it."

"Fine. Now here's another gem for you. I want Sanderson to be ignored. Do you understand?"

"Yes."

"When he's investigating, leave him alone. By that I mean when he's wandering around accomplishing nothing, don't bother him. Otherwise he isn't giving any orders. Don't give me that worried, helpless look. Either you do what I tell you or I'll have you locked up with Peterkin."

Quidler spread his hands. "Far be it from me to argue with you. What do you want me to do?"

"Get some help, find Peterkin and put him under lock and key."

"And if Sanderson and his agents interfere again?"

Bates smiled. "Get half a dozen workers to guard them. I mean it. If they try to let Peterkin out again, herd them all in one room and stick six of our best looking workers by the door."

"Okay. The Company is staffed by idiots. Where did they dig Sanderson up?"

"I don't know and I don't care."

Quidler went out and Bates picked up a mike and called a flunky up to her. He took his asbestos suit off before entering the booth.

"I need someone to do nothing but check the water level in the basement and report to me."

The kid went away to do his job and she settled back

in her chair to watch us. She was one good driver, could keep us on our feet while carrying on a conversation, and now that she was free she didn't push us past our limit but allowed us to work at individual paces. We were an essential part of the planet's labor force. A few miles away were the oil derricks that were all important, and our factory provided small parts for them. Without the derricks there would be no oil and without it all the planets in the system would become non-productive. Bates directed us to draw molten metal from the vat and fashion different shapes, items to be loaded into crates and transported to the oil fields. Which must be getting wet by now.

Chapter 18

The sawdust came from a supply dump a few miles away and I was conscripted to accompany a flunky there on a sled. It was my task to haul a canvas bag containing several hundred pounds of dust from the loading dock and attach it to the back of our vehicle.

The bruden dragged behind us as we returned to the compound, bouncing over the frozen waste, cutting our speed but remaining undamaged. Thus when we arrived at our destination the dust was ready to be placed in bags and laid against the buildings. It didn't seem to me that it was doing much good but then I had never possessed great foresight.

The flunky was lazy and sent me to bag with the other workers so that he wouldn't have to go back to the supply dump right away. If Quidler saw me standing idly about, he would naturally look for my driver and then it would mean another haul with the sled. Except that Quidler was nowhere in sight, which seemed strange to me.

Not curious enough to go and find out where he was, I didn't bag sawdust, either, but instead went to the library with the intention of making another recording for Bates. She needed to be told about kanalba and all the strange abilities of the frogs.

My presence in the halls wasn't especially unusual since they were narrow passageways perpetually clogged with people and workers. The only reason I attracted attention was because of my size but I guess everyone was accustomed to the sight of me so that I went my way unnoticed.

The library was quiet and empty and I stood just inside the entrance for a few moments thinking of all the intelligent ideas printed in the books lining the walls. Dumb ideas, too, I knew, but hoped the other kind outweighed them. Either way, I had no part or parcel with the written word and the place made me feel more ignorant than I probably was.

At least I was becoming proficient in the use of the computer and had switched it on to recording and was in the act of picking up the small mike attached to it when there was a disturbance at the door. I barely had time to scoot behind the machine and crouch down before Sanderson and one of his associates came into the room.

"Shut the door," Sanderson said in a low voice. "I don't think anybody saw us come in." He sat in a leather chair near the computer, stretched his legs and gave a loud groan.

The other man's name was Ledderman, a heavy-set young man with thick glasses and red hair. "If one more of those flunkies asks me what my assignment is I'll punch him out." He sat on a leather stool beside Sanderson and opened a bag lunch. Biting into a sandwich, he looked around. "Why do they have all these books here? Don't tell me those flunkies can read?"

"Not much better than the stiffs, I expect." Sanderson took an apple from his pocket and bit into it.

"What do you think?" said Ledderman.

"What about?"

"The piece they put in Peterkin's head back on Earth."

"What about it?"

Ledderman adjusted his glasses. "Is it working?"

"Of course it's working."

"Not if he killed that woman."

"He didn't kill her. Every time he reaches a fever pitch of emotion, that piece wipes his mind clean like his brain was dunked in formaldehyde."

"You hope."

Sanderson snorted. "You'd better do a little hoping yourself. This is an easy job with great pay."

"Yeah, you're right. But how can you be sure he didn't commit the murder?"

"What did I just tell you? That piece is a new experiment, a breakthrough, and he was the perfect guinea pig for it. He was due to go up for ninety-nine years if he so much as spit on the sidewalk. Emotions are thoughts too, you know, or at least they're accompanied by thoughts, or they're caused by thoughts. There's a little timer in the piece, like a thermometer or a weather vane, and when it heats up it means he's mad. If he gets too mad the piece releases electronic hunt-and-kill jolts. The brain cells of his anger are destroyed."

"How come he doesn't walk around looking like one of those stiffs?" said Ledderman, methodically eating his lunch.

"Because the hunt-and-kill is right on the button and gets rid of only the intense part of the anger. Just a couple of cells."

"Then he ought to be as cheerful as a clam."

"I doubt it. A guy like that is never happy. He's probably mean and mad all the time but now he can't climb to the top and jump off. Every time he works up a good rage the piece does its job."

Ledderman chewed in silence and then nodded. "That all sounds good," he said at last. "It still doesn't change the fact that there's a dead woman in the freezer waiting for passage home."

"There are dozens of people on the staff here. One of them is guilty."

"None of them has a criminal record. Only our boy Peterkin."

"Listen, that mechanical piece is working. I know it is. The biggest brains on Earth swear it can't fail."

"Then why are we here?"

"A precaution," said Sanderson. "They're about to implant those pieces in the heads of hundreds of psychotics in hospitals all over the world. This incident has to be no more than a coincidence."

"You'd better be sure before you give them the go ahead, otherwise your carcass will be served up later when the stuff hits the fan."

Sanderson belched, glanced angrily at the rows of books. "I'm already sure. One thing I don't worry about is my own judgment. If only that nag of a woman would leave me in peace for a few days. I've got to talk to Peterkin, really interrogate him. I need to make him angry and see how he reacts."

"It's too bad you don't outrank her."

"Nobody outranks her up here. Even if they did outrank her she wouldn't listen to them. If there's one thing I can't stand it's an overly confident broad."

"She's been burning up the communications lines between here and Company Headquarters, you know."

"It won't get her anywhere." Sanderson shook his head. "They won't want to jump on her so they'll string her along. We're here as long as we want to be and they'll tell her to go easy on us. She'll end up more confused than she's always been."

"I kind of like her. I feel sorry for her, in a way. She busts her coconuts and they lie to her. Why don't they just tell her the truth?"

"Because they never operate that way. This experiment is out of her jurisdiction. It's on a need-to-know basis."

"Murder isn't out of her jurisdiction."

Wiping his bald head, Sanderson said, "It's so bloody hot inside and so bloody cold outside. If you really want my opinion, that dead woman was done in by a stiff."

Ledderman laughed. "That sounds funny coming from you. You take all this time explaining to me how the piece in Peterkin's head prevents him from committing murder and then you say something like that. These people are stone-cold dead. In fact they aren't even people anymore. They're walking flesh motivated by machines. If any of them committed a crime it could only be at the instigation of a living person."

Instead of replying, Sanderson scowled at his feet stretched out in front of him. His boots were soaked through, likewise his pants up to his knees. Still he perspired, perhaps more because of his own thoughts than the weather.

"What about all the water?" said Ledderman. "There's a rumor going around that the frogs found a way to melt the ice. I heard that the comet that froze this dump in the first place is on its way back and will heat the surface to two hundred degrees."

"Nuts to rumors. Just plain nuts. As a matter of fact, it's suspected that a comet did tilt this world on its axis so that it froze over. That doesn't mean it actually happened or that the comet will ever come back this way. Besides, who cares? Stuff like that is measured in millions of years."

"Yeah, but what about the water?"

"The Company didn't tell me to worry about that and I don't plan to. If I had some high boots I wouldn't give it a second thought."

Ledderman crumpled the empty lunchbag and looked around for a wastebasket. There was one by the door. He arose, went over to it and disposed of his litter. "What now?" he said, glancing back at Sanderson.

"Keep on schedule and try not to foul anything up. We're not in a big hurry. I intend to notify the Company that it's okay up here but I want more time first. Just in case."

"Yeah, just in case."

"It's okay, though. I know it is." Sanderson stood up and followed Ledderman out of the room.

I realized it was all on tape, everything they had said. Coming out from behind the computer, I marveled at how inattentive people could be. All the time Sanderson and his man talked, a little green light on the computer had been blinking on and off.

Feeling more intelligent than I had ever felt in my life, I removed the tape from the cup and put it in my pocket, turned off the machine and followed a group of workers down the hall to the factory.

Going inside the work area and taking my place at one of the sealers without attracting Bates' attention was easy to do because workers were wandering all over the place. Evidently she was doing more woolgathering than usual and kept sending individuals to do specific jobs and then forgot to see the jobs through.

I sat down at a vertical machine beside Frye, wondering how I was going to get the tape onto the desk in the booth. I didn't want to wait until night but it looked as if I might have to. Unless, of course, I simply walked up there and told Bates I wasn't a stiff. My insides cringed at the thought. Never in my life had I been able to speak to a normal person and I couldn't do it now. Too many times medical people had discussed me in my presence as if I were deaf, dumb, blind and without feeling. It was an unfortunate complex but it was mine and I had to live with it.

Before the day was over I discovered that Quidler was locked in a room somewhere on the premises of the compound. Bates had a fit in the booth and everyone in the building heard it because she broadcast it everywhere. Too bad for her, there were no other mature people at her command now. The flunkies were kids intimidated by their own shadows and though they were willing enough to try and follow her orders, they were just as easily cowed by Sanderson and his people. Of course there was always Peterkin. Either Bates never considered him at all or else she silently consigned him to a limbo of uselessness.

Nothing got done. By that I mean Quidler stayed locked up because no one could find out exactly where he was imprisoned. Bates had the flunkies scour the building but Sanderson kept moving him around so that it was impossible to catch up with him.

Sanderson and Bates had a loud conversation via the intercom that wasn't fit to be listened to. The company agent swore he knew nothing of Quidler's whereabouts, protested being called a liar among other things and suggested that Bates call Headquarters if she didn't like what was happening. She did but couldn't get through because of stellar interference. Strange how the lines remained that way for the duration.

Chapter 19

It was two days before I could get into the factory booth and leave the tape on Bates' desk. I didn't know where her living quarters were, otherwise I might have tried a night foray and sneaked it into her room.

I don't know what emergency made her leave the factory the way she did that third day, and maybe there was really no emergency at all. It was possible that she simply got tired of directing workers. At the time there were no flunkies in the machine area to take over for her so she turned the driving computer to static, laid the hat on her desk and walked out.

We all stopped what we were doing and froze in our positions. As quickly as I could move, I got out of my chair, hurried between the machines and walked out into the hall with the intention of sneaking up an alternate set of stairs to the booth and stashing the tape.

It didn't take me long. I came out of the booth, closed the door and quietly went down the main stairs leading toward the factory entrance. Just as I was about to round a bend in the corridor, I stopped where I was and flattened myself against the wall. Bates was just out of sight where I couldn't see her, and she wasn't alone. Her strained voice sounded clearly in my ears.

"You!" she said. "What are you doing here? I want you to quit stalking me!"

I risked taking a fast look around the jutting partition and saw her standing in the shadows with her back close to the wall. Ten feet away from her stood Peterkin, his hands in his jeans pockets, a twisted smile on his face.

"It wouldn't do me much good to stalk someone like you, now would it?" he said. "You're so good at running I can hardly catch up."

"I'm not running!" Bates' back was really against the wall by then as Peterkin kept edging toward her, and then there was no place for her to go—she was enclosed on three sides by partitions.

"Maybe you've had enough, eh?" he said and half lunged at her.

At that instant I came out of my hiding place, squarely in front of him so that it was all he could do to keep from slamming into me. His eyes went wide with surprise as he caught his balance and backed away a few paces.

His glance flickered to Bates behind me and I saw a deep anger build in his expression. He was annoyed with me but he was positively enraged at her and as he kept backing stiffly away from me I knew why he hadn't killed her yet. He hated her too much. She made him too mad.

As I watched him, his expression went a little blank, bland, as if he momentarily lost his bearings. Then he was aware again, glaring at me with a touch of fear and a bit more ire, but the intensity of his emotions never approached their former level. The mechanical piece in his brain had done its job again.

It was plain to me that Sanderson's medical superiors had made a serious mistake. They fixed it so Peterkin would never again kill in a fit of passion, but what about cool, calculated murder? Kalla was being trained by Bates to take his place and he didn't want that. After all, who knew where he would be transferred? He couldn't predict how the penal authorities on Earth would interpret his getting booted out of his job. They might not be going along with the medical experiment at all. They might decide he had crossed the irrevocable line, haul him back into court and throw the book at him. How could he avoid all the possibilities his keen imagination presented to him? Simple. Stay cool. Kill Kalla, but not in a rage.

However he had figured it, he wanted to kill Bates, but he hadn't been able to do it. He wanted to do it now but his rage died away and stuck in his throat like a left-over taste.

He didn't even look at me. I was nothing. As far as he knew, Bates had an individual controller concealed in her pocket, or, conceivably, a flunky in another hallway was directing me. He meant to get me, all right, but he told me with a little smile that he had all the time in the world in which to do it.

I watched him and wondered why so many things in life were vastly different from how they appeared. Peterkin looked like a mild-mannered, clean-cut, amicable young man. His handsome face, wavy hair, strong figure and sublime demeanor were the biggest lie since Satan tempted Eve in the Garden.

He backed away from me, smiled, shrugged, suddenly wheeled and strode away with a cheerful whistle. I could hear the tune long after he was gone from sight.

With a little sigh of relief, Bates came out of her corner in a hurry. Taking hold of my arm, she said, "Hey!" She moved around in front of me but by that time I had my natural expression plastered on my face. She did have a controller in her pocket with which she could manipulate me in simple ways.

"Come on over here," she said. I let her lead me to a

chair and there I sat while she peered into my eyes and felt my head all over. Her hands were gentle.

"There's something crazy about you," she murmured, moving around me, probing, seeking. "More than once it has occurred to me that you're not the way you're supposed to be."

She seemed disappointed that her investigation turned up nothing out of the ordinary. A worker naturally showed all the vital signs, the same as I or anyone. Maybe my skin temperature was a little warmer than usual, but not too much so. The only way one could readly be sure a person was a worker was by checking the left armpit. The brand made in the hospital was an indelible mark. Bates did that now, pulled aside my shirt, raised my arm and looked at the round, white scar.

"Bloody dickens!" she said, dropping my arm and staring at me with a mixture of concern and resignation. "You're as dead as you'll ever be," she said. "Oh, well, I don't care if you can't hear me, you saved my hide from that walking psychosis and I appreciate it. Come along and be my guest."

I followed her back to the factory. At the entrance she paused, looked up at me and said, "I can't figure out where you came from, popping out in the hall like that? Who sent you there? Well, go along now, back to your machine and I'll keep extra watch on you. He'll probably try to do you harm. He has no logic or good sense."

I guess she was too distracted to see the tape right away. She went up into the booth, donned the metal hat and got us all to doing our thing again and for a while I felt almost sanguine. There were Frye and Flora working beside me, I felt physically well and Peterkin had been chased back into his hidey hole. I shouldn't have thought of him. It reminded me of LeMay and Zott and then I turned glum and blue all over again.

Of a sudden Bates began humming into the mike. It was late afternoon and the air was hot. The sounds coming down into the stifling work area were soft and kind of absent so I knew she had found my tape at last.

The humming continued, became more positive sounding and it wasn't long before she hauled a bottle of booze from a drawer and began swigging it down.

On and on she hummed, playing my tape over and over, sucking poison, thinking hard and maybe wishing she was a hapless housefrau with no worries, ambition or future.

It was a long time later that she relinquished the driver's hat to a flunky with instructions to take everybody to dinner.

"All except that big one," she said, and he took the workers out but left me behind. "Come on," she said to me. I waited at the foot of the stairs while she staggered down them, putting her life in jeopardy half a dozen times. They were steep and she was bombed.

With just the little controller in her pocket she dressed me for cold weather and led me outside to a sled. Overhead, it was dark gray and hostile-looking, lowering like an Earth sky before a heavy storm. It never rained on Land's End and now that the frogs had the engine I helped them steal, there was no need for any rain. Water was everywhere, shining in the dusky light in lakes, ponds, pools and puddles.

The sled worked fine, though. Bates sat on the seat and had me stand at the rails and look toward the horizon. She never said what she was hunting for.

"Just signal if you see anything unusual," she said, swaying. Hiccup. It wasn't much of an order. A real worker would have done a lot of staring at nothing and not much else.

The sled slid over the ice and through water like an amphibious craft. "I don't see how we can keep this up much longer," she said. "What do they think we are? I've told them this planet is seeping up around our ears, I've told them they ought to start evacuating. Stupid experiment. That's all they care about. Have you noticed how holy an experiment is in the eyes of humans? You can get away with almost anything as long as you stick that label on it."

She stood up and nearly fell out of the sled as it dipped into a wet culvert. "I'm going to catch my death out here," she said. She pounded me on the back. "Do you see anything besides ice and a lot of water? No, naturally you don't because that's all there is out here. The place belongs to the gray people and we had no right to just shove them aside." Hiccup. "Indians all over again. Do you know I have a lot of nightmares about Indians?"

She stopped the sled and got out. Slogging through slush, she stared up at the sky and yelled something I couldn't understand. Then she fell flat on her back.

I waited until I was certain she was unconscious before getting out and carrying her back. Putting her down, I returned the sled to the compound. I don't know why she went out in the first place unless it was to reassure herself that the water hadn't frozen all over again.

That it hadn't. The paths around the buildings were sunken at least a foot and a half and were filling up. Pretty soon walking wouldn't be a feasible mode of travel anymore.

She came to and seemed confused about where she was but it didn't last long and soon she ordered me into the building behind her. On the fourth level she stopped beside an apartment. "Sit down on the floor," she said to me. She needn't have spoken her wishes but only had to think them. Maybe I was getting on her nerves. Then again, maybe I wasn't. Patting me on the shoulder, she said, "There's a good sport. Just sit there and I doubt if anyone will come snooping around my door."

In a little while she had only partially sobered up and came out to take me to dinner. When we showed up side by side in the chow line, Mildred cast us a baleful eye.

"You takin' up with that one?" she said to Bates.

"What do you mean by that?"

"No offense, boss, but there's no reason for you to associate with this one." Taking a deep breath, Mildred gave me a triumphant stare and continued. "I been meanin' to tell you that this one is weird. Wanders around at all hours."

"Button your lip and ladle out the slop," said Bates, hiccupping loudly.

Mildred deflated like a balloon. Perhaps she was thinking how unlucky it was for her that the first time she found enough nerve to speak up about me, the boss had to be stewed.

"That's my life," she said. "A mess. All mixed up. Confusing, I'd say. Have your bleeping stiff for all the good it will do any of us. We're probably all going to drown in our beds."

Bates blinked, swayed, said, "Did you say something?"

"No, I didn't say nothing."

Taking no note of the fact that all the flunkies in the place moved away from us, Bates led me to a table and while I ate she picked at her food and muttered under her breath.

She wasn't completely herself, that was obvious to me when she took me to the bathroom with her. Normally a person wouldn't be caught dead anywhere with a worker, in a manner of speaking. Here Bates had not only shared a meal with me but we sat side by side in the head and engaged in a one-sided conversation.

She was overworked and harassed nearly beyond endurance because she had too much responsibility and not enough authority. If the communications channels between Land's End and Company Hq. on Earth didn't clear up so that she could get permission to evacuate, she would have to make the decision on her own. That meant they would probably hand her her head later. There were billions of dollars worth of equipment on the planet. Why junk an efficient project because of a little water, they would say? And they would be right. Later, when they sent a crew up to take a look, the place would probably be frozen solid again.

"I don't care about getting fired," she said to me. "And I hate to close down a good project. The other worlds need our oil. If we all evacuate, it'll take months to get production going once more, if everything turns out well.

If the water goes away. Where the devil is it coming from, anyhow?"

By nightfall she was cold sober and sent me back with the others. "Maybe I'll keep you for my mascot," she said, patting me on the arm. "We'll see. You'd make a swell bodyguard. I'll consider it."

My bunk in the dorm was damp. Not only that, the mattress was stained because it was too close to a leaky wall, so I picked up a guy a few beds away, deposited him on my bed and took his. That night I slept too soundly, otherwise I might have been able to save my friends. I'm not sure, though. They were so empty-headed.

I never got used to sleeping in the big open cubicle they called the dorm. There was no privacy and too much noise. Once in a while someone moved a leg or an arm, or they sat up in bed and snorted or coughed because the packs in their heads stimulated the wrong cells. It wasn't bad when one did it, but when they all moved, considerable sound was produced. At any rate, I lay on my back for a while worrying about everybody I knew when all of a sudden my lights went out and I dropped off to sleep.

The next thing I knew it was morning and a furor was taking place all about me. Flunkies were everywhere, making noise and looking white and scared. Bates was there trying to maintain order.

It seemed that sometime during the wee hours of the dawn someone chopped the devil out of the worker lying on my bunk. It was no secret that the weapons had been an axe and a butcher knife because they were there in plain sight lying on the breasts and bellies of Flora and Frye who were cozily tucked into bed. The place was a bloody mess and so were my two unfortunate friends.

The chopped-up corpse was taken away, the soiled bedding was disposed of, the bed and floor were scoured and then the workers were all marched up to the factory. I stood beside Bates as she ordered Flora and Frye to climb into the vat.

"I feel like an executioner," she said in a low voice. She took the time to glance at me but I don't think she could see the tears in my eyes because her own eyes glistened so much. "I want to apologize to all of you because this is my fault," she said. "I let it happen. Somehow I should have done something to avoid it." Her voice dropped even lower. "I don't want to do this but I must. The packs of these two women could be stuck on those same cells, you know, like maybe they're focused on the killing. They could do it again. I have no choice but to get rid of them."

Flora climbed those stinking struts and took her final dive in a dramatic fashion. There wasn't much noise until the soles of her feet disappeared in the bubbly liquid and then it was as if a big slab of bacon suddenly fried all at once. A puff of smoke shot toward the ceiling and that was the end of a harmless old lady. Her second end.

I couldn't bear to watch Frye. All the time she climbed the struts I kept hoping something would happen to save her, but it didn't. Bates couldn't change her mind and no one else cared. In fact no one else was around, except for the workers. The flunkies had all done a disappearing act so there was nobody to witness the end of my friend, other than Bates who gave a little gasp at the end to tell me it was over.

First LeMay, then Zott, then Flora and last of all Frye. All my friends. One way or another Peterkin had destroyed them. Now I was the only one left.

I thought he might be at least a little angry, wherever he was. He had planned to get rid of me, too, and he would have succeeded if my bunk hadn't been wet last night. As usual, the next move was his.

Chapter 20

Someone stole a large quantity of tranquilizers from the pharmacy; Quidler turned up after having battered his way out of a fourth-level room and Bates called the foreman in charge of the oil compound, then, when he came over, told him he would be a fool if he didn't evacuate his people from the planet.

Sal Verni was a big grease-spattered man with a reputation for bulling his way through interference and adversity. Towering over Bates outside our compound, he slammed a fist into a palm and said, "I came because you said you had something important to tell me. Is that it? You're advising me to pull my people out?" He looked as if he wouldn't mind slamming the fist in her face. "All because of a little water?" With a frown, he glanced around at the shallow lake that seemingly had no end. It wasn't just a little water he was talking about. The stuff was all over the place. In fact, the only things to break the glistening monotony were us and the ice dunes. As for Verni, he stood in it up to his knees. He took off his hat, brushed back his thick hair, raised a booted foot and kicked at the pesty stuff that wouldn't go away.

"When it's up to your armpits, what will you do?" said Bates.

"I'd like to see it get that high." Verni's voice was low and full of threat that wasn't directed at Bates but at circumstance. "Where did it all come from? Humans have been on this planet for more than three centuries. What's happening?"

"You have three hundred people and it will take you at

least two weeks to get them out. I'd appreciate it if you didn't delay. There's just the one steeple in our area. If both our groups try to board at the same time, some people might not make it."

Verni kicked more water on his way back to his sled. "I don't know what kind of advice you just gave me," he said over his shoulder. "I'll have to think it over."

"Naturally."

He stopped and turned. "What does Headquarters say? I'm going to call them on my own but what have they said to you?"

"Nothing. They aren't accepting direct calls. You can relay from Eden but that's all."

"That figures." Climbing onto his sled, Verni slowly pulled away. The water slopped across the runners but didn't reach up over the bed.

Sanderson came down the steps of the compound building with a glare at all the puddles he had to wade through to get to Bates. "You can't keep advising people to evacuate," he said. "Do you realize what you're doing to morale?"

"Must you sink in it up to your neck before you get the picture?"

"I have work to do here and I require a peaceful environment."

"To the devil with your experiment." Bates turned and signaled for us workers to follow her inside.

"What's that?" said Sanderson as she went up the steps away from him. "What did you say?"

"I said to the devil with your experiment. I don't want to hear anymore about it. I have important things on my mind. As a matter of fact, I want you to pack your gear and get out of here."

His expression turning a little vicious, Sanderson hurried up the steps after her, scooted around her and blocked the way. "I think you're forgetting who you're talking to."

"I don't think so. Get out of the way."

He was foolish to whip a gun out of his pocket. "I'm

taking charge here. I've got the authority, in my opinion. You're letting your gonads get in the way of your good sense. I say the water will recede."

As soon as I felt Bates probe for me with her mind through the driver's hat I broke ranks and walked up the steps. Sanderson looked up and up at me and his mouth was slightly agape as I reached out and took the gun away from him.

So much for a raw confrontation. He went inside to radio to Eden while the rest of us descended to the fourth level to do some salvage work. He would be frustrated and at his wit's end because none of the messages Eden relayed to Earth for him would be answered. No doubt HQ was up to its ears in conferences trying to decide whether or not to cancel Bates' evacuation decision. Already there were geologists on the way to investigate the water phenomenon and nobody high up wanted it broadcast that Bates had requested them weeks ago.

It was impossible for an iceworld to melt in a matter of weeks, months or even years. Such a process required the passage of millennia or at least centuries. Bates had to be off her shelf, probably driven round the bend by her husband's desertion, or so said one or two of the mouths of HQ. But, still. Let Verni and the oil people curse and rage but let them get out. There were plenty of shuttles moored in the steeple ready to take them to the depots of Eden which was the world nearest to Land's End. The oil wells would have to remain capped until the situation stabilized. As for the straggler colonists from the domed city who still hadn't debarked, the order for them to evacuate was in effect. All other commands had received the same order and were in the process of packing up. The factory compound would be the last to go. Somehow that seemed only just.

In the meantime Quidler related a few terse items to Bates. "I had to get out of that room or drown." He looked beat and exhausted. "Sanderson didn't even see to it that I was fed. I was afraid that I was going to starve. Either he completely forgot me or he's nuts."

"He's deeply into his scientific experiment. That's supposed to explain everything."

"If you take away all his guns he'll shut his mouth and do as he's told."

"I intend to get them," she said.

"What about Peterkin?"

"I'm glad you asked. Take a couple of workers, go find him and lock him up."

"Sanderson will just let him out."

"If he tries I'll lock him up too." Bates turned to a flunky and ordered him to go downstairs and check the water level.

"I told you it's coming into the fifth floor," said Quidler.

"I'm hoping it was just some leakage from upstairs plumbing. If it's really up to the fifth we've got a worse problem than I thought."

Two feet of water stood in the fifth level which meant that all of the workers and most of the flunkies had to pitch in to salvage what they could. Meanwhile Quidler and I and another worker went away to hunt for Peterkin.

He was in the library with Sanderson and three agents. Quidler remained by the door and listened for a few minutes before going in.

"Then how do you explain it?" Sanderson was saying.

Peterkin's responses were straightforward, earnest, calm and a pack of lies. "I can't really, no more than anyone else can. I think she jumped all over me as a suspect because I wasn't interested in any hanky panky."

"What?" said Sanderson. "What did you say?"

"She's been here awhile, and I guess she gets a little lonely. I'm a family man, as you know, and though I've been guilty of a couple of indiscretions, cheating on my wife wasn't one of them."

"Good Heavens, that never occurred to me!" Sanderson wasn't being facetious. He clearly meant what he said. He hadn't suspected that Bates' accusations were based on anything but frank logic even though he liked to believe she was overly emotional.

Neither had I. If Quidler hadn't chosen that moment to barge into the library he would have been surprised—for I leaned against the door with the intent of breaking the hinges.

Sanderson was displeased to see us; Peterkin seemed amused and the agents with them drew their weapons.

"You'd better blast away, otherwise we're taking your guinea pig and locking him up," said Quidler. "He's a killer."

"He's nothing of the sort!" said Sanderson. "It's impossible for him to kill." He looked at me as I came to a halt beside him. I think he shuddered. "This place is staffed with backwater personnel!" he said. "Can't you let me alone to do my job?"

"Sorry." Quidler placed a set of handcuffs on Peterkin and led him away. At the last minute I turned back into the library, crossed to the agents and relieved them of their guns. I thought one of them was going to shoot me but he only went pale, stiffened and dropped his weapon into my hand. I put them in my back pockets, walked all the way to the end of the building to a stairwell and looked down at the rising black water. One by one I dumped the guns and watched them sink.

On Bates' order Quidler took Peterkin to the glass booth in the factory and tied him to a chair. Meantime I joined my untalkative associates in the work area below. They were there to shut the factory down, demobilize machinery, cool the vat, carry a few essential machines out to the foyer. We were on ground level and there were two more floors above us but Bates wasn't confident that the water wouldn't eventually flood those, too. Of course if it did that, the machines would be lost anyway.

"This is stupid," Peterkin said to Quidler. He looked tired but not particularly upset. I think he was enjoying all the attention he was getting.

"So are you, telling such whoppers to that fool Sanderson. As if Shirley ever gave you any encouragement! In fact she wanted to get rid of you right from the start. You may be pretty but your personality is lousy."

"I tell Sanderson things like that to get him off my neck for a minute. He's always at me with his idiotic questions. I've had it with him."

"And I with you. Shirley will be along shortly. If you bother her with your mouth I expect she'll shove a gag in it."

"Wait, I want you to do me a favor. Before you go, do you see that big stiff down there? The woman? The ugly one?"

"What of it?"

"You've got to get rid of her for me. Toss her in the vat or weigh her down and throw her into the water. No, no, don't look at me like that, you must do it! She has a hex on her. If you don't destroy her we're all done for."

"You're nuts!" said Quidler, his tone one of wonder. "Blooming, bloody fruity!"

"Listen to me. She's an evil one like the other four she roomed with. I got rid of them but now I'm tied up and can't take care of her. You have to do it for me."

Quidler was about to leave. Now he turned back. "What do you mean you got rid of them? What did you do?"

"I made one climb up over the vat, I infected a second with green fungus and the last two were executed by Bates because they chopped up that worker."

"You're pitiful, that's what you are. Your brain is full of gangrene. Just you sit there and go over all your problems in your mind, and see if you can't come up with a decent solution to all of it, like, say, cutting your own throat."

Quidler went out and Peterkin sat up there humming to himself. Now and then he worked his chair closer to the glass and stared down at me. The driving machine was on automatic so that the workers were immobile so I sat quite still and stared back at him. His humming was weird and crazy, soft and then wild, absent and then hurried, as if the mind responsible for the sounds operated on abnormal frequencies.

The heat nearly drove Sanderson away when he ventured into the work area, but his experiment meant a great deal to him so he braved the confines and the temperature, scurried between the machines and hastened to the side exit. I think he would have fainted from sheer terror if the door had been locked. The discomfort plus the sight of the workers bent over or in mid-stride were too much for him and he hurtled against the partition with a sob in his throat. With haste he shut it behind him and climbed the stairs to the booth.

"Ah, it's you," Peterkin said as he came in.

"Don't sound so down, my boy. I know you didn't kill that girl and I'm probably the only one who does know it."

"Untie me."

"Surely, surely." Sanderson took out a pocketknife and freed Peterkin. "Now we can have another rap session. They're important, you know. Everything is on tape."

"That's good. Of course when I listen to them again I'll cut out a lot of the dumb stuff you said."

"Eh?" Sanderson's normally puzzled look was plastered all over his face as Peterkin advanced upon him with the knife. He yelped like a puppy when the blade bit into the fleshy part of his upper arm. In bewilderment he stared from his torn shirt to Peterkin's face and back again. "Why did you do that?" he said in a broken voice.

The response was casual. "To see if the knife was any good. It isn't very, but it'll do. Turn around and go down into the factory. Tut, tut, don't balk and don't give me any kind of a hard time. My patience is running out. You have that effect on me. They should have sent someone else. Your personality grates on my nerves."

Peterkin looked happier than I'd ever seen him. And more handsome. The dampness in the air curled his hair and made him appear more angelic than he normally did.

Sanderson did as he was told and tried not to swallow his tongue. He kept trying to speak but only wheezes came from his throat. At last he managed some partially intelligible phrases. "I don't . . . what is . . . this won't . . ."

"Shut up." Opening the door of the booth, Peterkin

shoved him down the stairs. They were steep and I was surprised when Sanderson made it to his feet and came on inside the factory. Peterkin stabbed him in the side of the neck with the knife and when he cried out he was kicked until he fell.

"Get up, Mr. Scientist. Get up, you bloody pest! What a bellyfull I've had of you!" Suddenly Peterkin straightened and laid a gentle finger to his own cheek. "Careful, boy," he cautioned, as if he were speaking to someone else and not himself. "Those pills will keep you from getting too overwrought, but you'll still have to watch it." A foot lashed out and caught Sanderson who was scrambling between the machines on his hands and knees.

"Not that way!" Peterkin glanced in my direction and grinned. "We want to stay away from Miss Gruesome over there. She's hexed and I don't aim for her to be interfering with me." Again he kicked Sanderson. "Very clever, that machine your friends put in my head. The only thing wrong about it was that they neglected to ask for my permission to do it." The foot lashed out. "How would you like it if a bunch of butchers hacked your head open and stuck a piece of machinery in your brain?"

I don't know how much of the picture Sanderson had by then but it was enough for him to be terrified. He lay on his back in the stifling heat, stared up at his persecutor and felt of his bleeding neck at the same time. His face was cut and bruised where he had been kicked against the machines. He wasn't that small a man and I think he could have made a good fight of it if Peterkin's savagery hadn't demolished his spirit. I kept expecting him to do some lashing out of his own, but he never did. Unable to resist, he sprawled and waited to see what fate held in store for him.

"Get up," Peterkin said. "Go on and do as I say. Pick up that chain and lock on the shelf there by the wall." His foot lashed out and Sanderson moved and did as he was told. "Chain that big stiff to her machine. I want her unable to move. Do it or I'll kill you."

Frightened, shaking, Sanderson ran the chain around my waist, looped it about the machine nearest to me and pulled it so tightly I was jammed up against the metal. The lock was fit to the loops and I was imprisoned before I had made up my mind what to do.

"Now get back over here to me," he was told.

Suddenly there was a noise outside the work area. The machines were all off and no one made a sound as Bates opened the outside door in the hall and went up the stairs to the glass booth. With a smile on his face Peterkin sneaked to the exit, opened it and silently followed her up. From his pocket he removed a key. At the last moment he shoved her inside the booth and locked her in. Then he came back down into the factory to deal with poor Sanderson.

I never wonder much about why criminals do the things they do. Obviously they do them because they like it.

I was too close to the wall for Bates to see me from the booth. While I tried to break my chain with my bare hands, she plastered herself against the glass up there, banged on it and yelled at the top of her lungs for Peterkin to stop.

By the time Sanderson was done he was nearly naked and bleeding from a hundred shallow stab wounds. The skin on Peterkin's face and neck was bright red and peeling. I guess the tranquilizers he had stolen were doing a good job of keeping his rage from reaching certain levels or temperatures. I don't know. He was as evil as a devil and what he did to Sanderson was an act only a hellion could have enjoyed.

Time and again Sanderson tried to get away from the vat only to be driven toward it again by his malevolent foe. The flesh on his face boiled and once more he tried to save himself by getting away from the heat. Peterkin was there every time, everywhere, slashing with the knife, punching, kicking. Back, back, Sanderson was driven toward the vat and each time he approached it he began to roast like a slab of beef. His back oozed steadily, red tears trailed down his cheeks, the flesh on his neck split and bled. Peterkin didn't look much better and only his savagery kept him going.

At last it became evident to Peterkin that no matter how much punishment he inflicted upon Sanderson, the other man wasn't going to oblige him by climbing the struts and leaping into the vat.

Meanwhile Bates had collected her wits and thought of a few weapons she had to hand. Grabbing up the driver's hat, she jammed it on her head and ordered the workers to stop Peterkin.

It was too bad she didn't do it sooner. It was too bad I hadn't acted before the chain was put on me. Everything was too bad. By then Peterkin had hoisted Sanderson up by a pulley cable and was swinging the flailing body out over the infernal cauldron. Maybe it had been too late for Sanderson long before he swung over the bubbling fluid. I don't think he could have survived the damage he had already sustained. A worker came up behind Peterkin and hit him on the head with a fist. The pulley cable slipped from the limp grasp and Sanderson was delivered down into his fiery tomb. I think he was dead before he landed. He didn't even cry out.

Chapter 21

I was so disgusted with the flunkies that when they lost contact with us workers and my companions fell down, I maintained my seat and tried not to swear out loud. We were in a boat and there were twenty of us, fourteen civilians, two flunkies, three workers and Peterkin. The craft had to be put together from parts because travel to the launching steeple by sled was impossible. The water was six and a half feet deep and getting deeper hourly.

The boat was made of canvas and lined with rubber. Wooden railings had been fashioned into the lining and the thing was propelled by two sled motors attached to the stern. The flunkies had a guide beam but misread it so that when we approached the steeple it was from the west side where there were no entrances.

The sky was gray and a wind had held us back during the entire trip causing us to make poor time. Surprisingly it was a warm wind, almost hot. That was odd but it was good because if the water had been cold a great many more people would have died. For instance, Sal Verni made several more trips to our compound in his sled before deciding to do what he was told and move his people out. He always ended up soaked. Everyone who went out of doors these days always ended up soaked. Only the dunes and the hidden ground were cold while everything else was too warm.

The flunkies panicked because they were young and because they were scared to death. We were up against an immense side of the steeple and would have to travel several more miles to get around to the north side. Meanwhile the passengers, all except Peterkin, were indulging in some old fashioned terror. He sat in a secure corner bulwarked by what he probably considered expendable flesh and observed the goings on with a slight smile. Naturally he didn't want to be taken back to Earth where there seemed to be a paucity of mercy and understanding regarding his behavior, so he bided his time and waited for fate to either kill or deliver him.

At least we had plenty of lanterns with which we tried to guide the boat along the steeple wall. There was a narrow catwalk built into the framework and a couple of the civilians left us and clambered up to it. I didn't think it was much of a choice. The water might still be relatively shallow but king-sized waves were gathering and crashing against the structure. If the pair didn't get washed away, they had a good six miles of struggling before they reached the nearest door.

The waves hit us and sent us thudding against the metal wall. A lamp was knocked from a flunky's hand and fell overboard. The two workers, left on their own, were too inert to help themselves. Though they sprawled on the bottom of the boat most of the time, they were subject to gravity, flopped about and were even hurled upon the railings now and then. Peterkin had been sitting quite calmly but all of a sudden, as one of the workers bounced against the rail beside him, he grabbed the body and tipped it over the side. No one complained any more about that than anything else. Everybody was screaming.

The sky grew darker while the wind increased in velocity. It seemed as if there was more water inside our craft than outside. A few of us began using our caps to bail. It was too dark for me to worry about being seen, and besides, at that point I doubted if anyone would have cared.

The wind took us, slammed us hard against the steeple so that the side of our flimsy boat bent inward. At the same time a wave picked up the stern and dumped everybody out. As I went overboard I took hold of the rail and didn't let go.

The boat righted itself and I was left hanging half in and half out of the water. Someone floundered to my left and finally found the hand I offered. Spitting and choking, my old friend Mildred came up out of the deep to catch a close glimpse of my face. Her breath whistled in her throat for a moment or two before her eyes rolled back in her head. Getting behind her, I shoved her to safety, intending to grab the rail again and follow her inside, but a wave caught me in the face and threw me backward.

There was absolutely nothing I could do to help myself. A poor swimmer to begin with, I lay on my back while the steeple seemed to dance away on the heaving surf.

At about the instant that it occurred to me that I was going to drown, a tiny hand clutched my arm. Another second passed and then the smiling face of Felix was there in front of me, like a seal or a porpoise. More hands gripped me and bore me upward.

"A friend in need," said Felix. He motioned for his companions to let go of me and then they levitated me across the water. It was like floating on wet air.

They took me back to the boat which was now far off course. Putting me in it and leaving me in safety, they went away to hunt for survivors. It took a couple of hours but they managed to round up nearly everyone and shoved us back to a steeple entrance.

There were some sorry-looking people who were finally delivered over to the launch personnel. The great doors were opened, a ramp fell in front of us and all the civilians were taken aboard. On a higher level the shuttle sat in its pit ready to blast off for Eden. It contained most of the oil people and had room for our small group.

One of the flunkies and Peterkin was missing. As the stragglers filed up the ramp and away, one of them turned to look back at the boat held fast beside the open doors. It was Mildred. For the first time in my life I was surprised out of my wits. Half drowned, terrified, sick and exhausted, my acquaintance from the cafeteria raised a hand to me and waved good-bye. I could swear she was even smiling.

I couldn't blame the last surviving flunky for what he did. Maybe he had some suspicions that I wasn't exactly as I should have been and that it wasn't just a stiff he was abandoning, but he was all human and convinced that this was his last chance for life. At the final moment, when the ramp was being pulled up, he left me there alone in the boat and scrambled inside. I could see him peering out a porthole as my craft began drifting away. Bates had ordered him to return to the compound with the workers. Now he was gone and there was just me. There were also howling winds and angry water. So much for a faithful servant.

It made me bitter, a familiar feeling. All my life people had been dumping me. At least I still had my frog friends.

No sooner did the boat begin rocking than Felix climbed aboard and steadied it.

"Yeah, I know," I said glumly. "Kanalba."

"How you been, kid?"

"Lousy."

"Kanalba."

"I already said that." I looked back at the steeple and wondered where Peterkin was. "You missed some bodies," I said.

"We apologize. The environment is not all that familiar to us."

"Don't kid me. You're fish and you've always been fish."

"In a way, though it was as much a surprise to us as it was to you. You are the savior of our world and our people. What can we do for you?"

I waved a hand to indicate that I was beyond help. But I was curious. "What are you eating these days?"

"Beneath the ice lives a multitude of aquatic life. There are great openings now through which we can swim. Did you know we are basically vegetarian?"

I grunted. "You're also naked," I said.

His little gray face lit up as he laughed. I could see him quite easily though the sky had grown darker. He seemed to carry a faint illumination inside him, somewhat like the pools on the oases. "We have no more pain. No more bleeding. We touch one another in the water and it feels fine. Incidentally, we're finished with your atomic engine. I swtiched it off and am prepared to return it to you."

I didn't know whether to laugh or not. "Thanks. I guess I don't really mind what's happening as long as none of my people die needlessly."

"No big harm done?"

"A big harm done to a lot of egos and pocketbooks."

Looking at me steadily he said, "But especially to your own ego which grows smaller daily."

"I never had much to begin with so it's no great loss."

"My people disagree. We never believed we would ever look at the face of kanalba. You are kanalba."

"You mean fate? I'm just the only person who ever took the trouble to find out what you were like."

The boat slid across the water like a sled over ice. I don't know if there were any other frogs near us. It was too dark to see. Felix sat on the bow railing in a relaxed posture as if he didn't have a care in the world. He hadn't changed a bit, though his environment certainly had. Little and sleek, he seemed far more hapless and vulnerable than he was.

"Will you do something for the humans?" I said.

"You have only to ask."

"Whenever any boats leave the different compounds to try and reach the steeple, will you send your friends to help them arrive at their destination?"

"Consider it done."

It didn't surprise me too much when the factory compound suddenly loomed in the dimness. In a few minutes I was delivered to the front door, which would soon be threatened by the water. Before I stepped out, I turned and said, "Do you have any high places that you think might not be submerged after all the ice melts? I don't mean the steeple or the derricks. Something of your own."

"Not many. One or two, perhaps. Why?"

"I think it would be fitting if you took that atomic engine and stuck it on a high peak. Sort of as a memento."

"Or a joke?" Felix grinned. "I'll do it."

He went away and I wondered if I would ever see him again. The ridge on his back rippled upon the surface for a moment and then he was gone like a sea denizen, a small, benign man whose world had turned hard and hostile around him, threatening to extinguish him and his kind. How must his ancestors have felt when the first humans came and began setting up all their booming machinery? Had any of those humans cared enough to try to communicate with the species they called frogs? I was sure they had. My kind were too full of curiosity to let an entire race go ignored. Maybe they experimented with the frogs like they did Earth animals. It wouldn't have gotten them anywhere and that's probably why they quit. The only human who was able to communicate with Felix and his people was me, not because I was kanalba or anyone important but because I was born a freak and had a machine in my brain.

The last waning light showed me an ocean that grew calm with nightfall. It was a good place for fish, with plenty of food, plenty of space, plenty of warmth and with not a speck of dry land anywhere.

Shrugging, I went inside the compound. In the back of my mind I still wondered what had happened to Peterkin.

Chapter 22

Doctor Garrett was a middle-aged, myopic man who looked as if he didn't believe he would be able to satisfy Bates' curiosity or interest in me.

The three of us were in the clinic where Garrett was attempting to prove whether I was alive or dead, not with much enthusiasm. Since he hadn't unlimited facilities in his place of business, he abandoned most of his instruments and attempted to do the proving with his mouth.

"I don't see why the mere fact that she and the boat came back from the steeple should upset you so much," he said. He sounded impatient and harried, as if the noise of the departing crowds in the halls made him also wish to be gone. "The obvious answer is that one of the staff returned with her."

"That doesn't jibe with the call I received from the launch people. She was the only one left in the boat when the doors were closed. The boy with her finked out at the last minute."

With a frown, Garrett tapped my knee to see if I had any reflexes. I had never had many before so my leg didn't jerk. "Seems cold-blooded for them to shut her out even if she isn't a real person," he said. "To leave her like that."

"Is she?" said Bates. "Dead, I mean?"

"Certainly she's dead! What do you take the company for?" The doctor raised my arm and pointed to the brand. "There's your proof."

"Don't give me that. You'll have to do better."

Garrett laid down his stethoscope and sighed. "I don't know why I'm using this blamed thing anyhow. Of course her heart is beating." He sat down in a chair behind his desk and looked at Bates. "You need more appreciation for the art of science, and that's no contradiction or play on words. The pack took this large and unprepossessing corpse and made it a functioning unit, not a machine but an operating mass of flesh and bones. She has everything a human being has except for one thing: the ability to think. She doesn't, therefore she isn't."

"Why doesn't she have dark rings around her eyes?"

"Probably because there was very little time lapse between her death and the surgical implant. Do you know that if you leave a corpse alone the blood in it will make it turn black? A matter of time has simply made a big difference in her appearance. She eats, breathes, eliminates and works. That's about it."

For a moment Bates was silent. Then she said, "You're hedging. Your logic doesn't tell me how you determine whether or not a person is dead or alive."

"How else but in an obvious manner? If the brain is dead and there are no vital signs, then a person is dead."

"What about her? You're assuming she's dead because she has a brand in her armpit and a machine in her head. I tell you there's something strange about her."

Garrett reached out and took my hand. "She feels warm. I admit to you that she looks more alive than most of them but then they all look somewhat alive. When they aren't flat on their backs they don't look dead because that's their natural position as far as our subconscious is concerned. I can tell you that this woman bore the brunt of a lot of ridicule and pity while she was alive. How tall is she, seven feet and more? Not only that, she's built like a football player and while she doesn't exactly look like a gargoyle she has a face not even a mother could love. Without knowing a thing about her I'd hazard a guess that her mental capacities were quite limited. Life couldn't have been much of a picnic for her but I swear to you that her life ended some time before she was brought here to this planet. She has no name, no background, no personality, no ego. She doesn't exist. Her spirit is gone. She's a corpse activated by a fantastic little machine in her head. As for you, my overworked lady, you've been among the dead too long. It's time you quit this job and went back among the living."

"Except that if I depend upon your judgments I'll never be able to tell the difference without checking armpits." Bates took my hand and pulled until I stood on my feet. "Come on, kid, let's go chase tigers," she said.

"What about Peterkin?" said Garrett.

"Still missing and unaccounted for. I hope he's floating under the water out there somewhere."

"Isn't that a little drastic?"

"Not when I consider the alternatives." She led me down a crowded hallway, up a staircase and into the library. Using the driving machine in her pocket, she had me sit in a chair. "I don't know what to do with you or about you," she said to me. "I only know I owe you a lot. You stay here where you won't get into any trouble and when I figure out what to do I'll come back for you. Okay?"

She looked at me from the doorway. "I think he's right and you're just a nice, big stiff. The company wouldn't do such a thing, couldn't make such a mistake. They don't put packs in people who haven't died." Giving me a sad stare, she went out.

I sat for the longest time because I wanted to obey her

but it got to be a drag looking at all those books so I got up and went outside. The hallway was empty. Everyone was on the floor below, making ready to leave. Not much was involved in presenting oneself at the main entrance for a boat seat. There was no packing, no luggage, no preparation, just boats and room in them for bodies. Living ones. I had no doubt that if the water kept rising at its present rate there wouldn't be time for everyone to be salvaged. If it came to push and shove, the workers would be left behind.

With nothing to do and no one to order me around, I did what came naturally, wandered and snooped into things as I waited for fate to make of me a dud or someone significant.

I strolled down into the factory to see how damp the floor was becoming. It didn't seem possible that water could seep through solid concrete so I investigated until I found some cracks in a corner through which a solid stream flowed.

The silence of the room filled me with a sense of unease. I walked over to the vat and marveled that the heat didn't leap out to hurt and drive me away. Most of the metal was gone from the bottom of the tub and now formed a scummy dark residue no more than a foot deep. It was still hot and would require several more hours to completely cool but for the time being it was something for me to look at and puzzle over. It had been such an object of pain and destruction in my experience that I couldn't quite believe it would shortly be neutralized.

Something fell in the glass booth above my head but when I looked up I saw no one and nothing out of the ordinary. Backing away from the vat, I turned to my machine and switched it on. There was no juice flowing through that particular line, no sound, no action. The thing was as dead as Garrett believed I was.

The place was so quiet it gave me the spooks. In fact it was too quiet. With a start I realized there should at least be someone out in the hallway, either below the glass booth or in the north end. Thinking I would go and investigate, I passed by the vat and began winding my way between the machines and tables toward the door. At that moment I had no inkling of anything wrong, just a feeling of strangeness.

The truth didn't even dawn upon me when the door opened and five workers came in. I did stop where I was, thereby lessening their initial advantage somewhat, but it still didn't occur to me that anything was unusual. I simply stood where I was while they came at me. As far as I was concerned there was a flunky outside in the hall who would soon make his presence known. Perhaps there was a machine or tools too valuable to leave behind that the workers had come to retrieve.

It was what I thought until nobody else came through the door and it hit me that I was the intended destination of the five. The intended victim. They were going to beat my head in and stuff my remains down the nearest convenient drain.

One of them took a wild swing at me with a length of pipe he picked up from a table. I had always been slow and it wasn't until then that I truly realized what was happening. I got my arm up in time to protect my face and the weapon came down on my shoulder in about the same spot where the last pair of would-be assassins had clobbered me. The pain went all the way down my side, leaving a white-hot sensation that radiated across every rib and bone I owned.

I had to take the time to whirl and look up at the glass booth because I knew now that the sound I had heard had been significant. As I did so, another worker took me by the neck. I shook him off, brushed my hair out of my eyes and stared up at the gleeful face of Peterkin. He was up there, all right, wearing the big driver's hat, comfortably ensconced in the room and not drowned at all as I had supposed. How had he saved himself? I had no idea. Maybe he hung onto the steeple catwalk, waited for a boat full of refugees and then confiscated it once it was abandoned.

Not that it made a great deal of difference to me then

how he had managed to survive. Just knowing he was up there in the booth in command of five large workers was sufficient knowledge for me to lose any optimism I might have had. The first thing I did was try to influence my adversaries with my thoughts but I had no effect on them. They weren't listening to me but were tuned in on Peterkin, whether because he had diddled with their packs I didn't know.

The man who hit me with the pipe tried it again but I ducked the blow, ran past the vat and turned to face them. The last one didn't even bother to come near me but minded Peterkin's urgings, crossed to the end of the room and began tossing tools at me. He was strong and his aim was good. A wrench hit me in the back of one knee and threw me forward just as the stiff who was swinging the pipe came at me again. I kicked him in the thigh and sent him stumbling away.

Quickly I climbed the side of the vat and began walking around the rim. It was hot but my boots had heavy soles. I didn't need a great deal of support and only had to touch the struts lightly to maintain my balance. The two healthy workers climbed up after me, began following me around the rim. One stumbled and fell, grabbed the rim and tried to hold on but gradually he lost his grip and slid down the sloping wall into the dark dregs at the bottom. They weren't white hot by any means but they were metal and still more in a fluid than a solid state. His legs were burned off below the knees.

Meanwhile the man behind me reached out and tried to grab me. I knocked him off the rim onto the floor. The one with the pipe took a swipe at my legs but I jumped fast enough so that the bare edge hit me. I felt the flesh below my knee break, felt the blood begin to flow.

As I jumped to the floor, one came at me with a chain at the same time that I was hit in the back of the head with a flying tool. I turned toward the chain wielder just as he caught me full in the face. My nose went out of joint, some teeth came loose, I lost the vision in one eye as the brow caved in. Still I wasn't done and went for him, took the chain and wound an end about his neck. Dragging him past the vat to a machine, I tied him to it, up high so that he would choke. If he went for a while without air, the pack in his brain would shut down and that would be the end of his aggression.

They were relentless because the man driving them was relentless. The one who had lost his lower legs managed to drag himself up to the rim of the vat, hauled himself over, dropped to the floor and began crawling toward me. He was no real threat, though, since all I had to do was step out of his way. A healthy one was punching me steadily with his fists while another took a good grip on his pipe and aimed a powerful swing at me. Had it landed, I think it would have killed me on the spot or made such a mess of me that they could have finished me at their leisure.

I practically fell getting out of the way. The guy behind me, the one who was taking such delight in punching me out, was fairly tall and the pipe caught him on the side of the head. It crushed him like an egg. Even before he fell, the pack in his brain flew out and rolled across the concrete.

It was too much trouble getting up. I couldn't see very well; there was a cauldron of agony threatening to boil over inside me, besides which one of my legs didn't want to work. The man standing over me didn't have his pipe anymore for it had flown from his hands when he brained his companion. With my good arm I dragged him down beside me, avoided his clawing hands and leaned my elbow against his windpipe. When I felt it give way I let him go. He thrashed about for a while and then lay still.

That left the big one who had given off throwing things and was running toward me with a claw hammer held high. Maybe Peterkin thought the tool could do more damage if it were hurled. It hit me in the side when I didn't move quickly enough.

I managed to crawl beneath a machine so that by the time the guy reached me and started kicking, I had a partial protection. He grabbed up a loose chain from a table and lashed me with it as I crawled across the aisle to another machine. Somewhere he found a second hammer, knelt and tried to hit me through metal legs. Reaching out, I grabbed him by the neck and yanked him toward me so that his skull hit against the steel. A hole appeared in the top of his head but the pack wasn't damaged so the blow hadn't much effect on him.

Again he knelt to grip me. I took hold of his throat with one hand, squeezed as hard as I could until he began to thrash. Still holding onto him, I clambered to my knees, let go and grabbed up a blowtorch off a nearby table. It came on as I punched the switch. In the act of trying to catch his breath, squatting and hanging on, the worker stared at me while his head burned away. He didn't fall until the pack was affected.

Feeling like a dead woman for the first time since I had arrived on Land's End, I staggered to my feet. He was still up there, Peterkin was, still in the booth cursing his bad luck and no doubt trying to think of other things he could do to me. I didn't care if he had a dozen guns, all I could think of was getting across the factory floor to the door. I wanted to climb those steps, rip open the glass booth and get my hands on his throat.

He probably guessed my intent but he didn't plan allowing it to happen. Standing with his face pressed to the glass, he took note of the poor headway I made toward the exit. In fact I fell once and lay still for quite a while, perhaps giving him the courage to think of trying to make an escape, but then I raised up and stumbled onward. Before I went through the door I picked up a welder's shield, held it in front of my upper body. I didn't bother turning the doorknob but rammed my way through just as he came out of the booth.

On the bottom step I braced the shield in case he decided to empty his gun at me. He surprised me by jumping all the way from the landing squarely onto my metal protection. My already unsteady legs went out from under me and I slammed back against the wall. He was too panicked to stay and finish the job. Maybe by then he had come to believe I was invincible.

I didn't feel anything but my pain. With the shield lying across my lap, one leg twisted back under me, I sprawled against the wall and watched while he scrambled to his feet and raced away down the hall.

Chapter 23

For the first time in my life I was being fussed over, really fussed over, and I didn't like it, not that Doctor Garrett was crazy about it either. When Bates had four workers cart me into the clinic, he took one look at me and then at her and said, "You're kidding!"

"Furthermore, I want her looking pretty when she comes out of here," she said toward the end of her emotional response. Then she went off to see what she could do about the war Quidler and Peterkin waged on the lower level.

Garrett had already made a lot of remarks about how I didn't feel pain because I wasn't even there, only my husk, but his hands were intent and kind enough as he patched me up the best he could. There was nothing to be done about my front teeth as they were lying somewhere in the rubble and water below and couldn't be found. He straightened my nose and packed one nostril, lifted my bent brow so that I could see again, stitched my head, put my shoulder in a light case and wrapped my left leg.

Standing back away from me and surveying his work, he said, "My dear, if it was ever possible in this wide universe to make you even half pretty I'd do it and earn myself the Nobel for performing a miracle." He reached out and patted my good shoulder. "Just be glad you're dead."

I had about had it with him. I was compelled to do it, had to give him a deliberate wink before standing up and limping out of his office. He didn't faint, I'll say that for him, and he didn't yowl or gasp, he just gave me a disbelieving stare and shook his head a couple of times as if it had filled up with wool. The last I saw of him, he was rummaging in a cabinet marked, "Tranquilizers."

I wasn't heading out to do any battling. My fighting days were over for the time being for I was a walking bruise, creaking at the joints, tattered at the seams, rocky, feeble and scarcely able to hobble down the hall and locate a decent seat to witness the war below.

The arena had been a gymnasium before doomsday and was large enough to contain both armies. Quidler was holding the fort, in a manner of speaking, fighting off Peterkin's forces and preventing them from climbing the stairs to the top level where Bates was engaged in helping refugees through a window, down a makeshift ramp and into waiting boats. This was the last stand and the cooks and flunkies weren't reluctant about grabbing anything that floated to get them to a seaworthy craft. The boats were everywhere in the water, some moored by lines, others adrift with their distress lights frantically blinking.

It seemed that I was never going to get the vat completely out of my immediate experience. The factory had flooded while the thing accidentally heated up again and the ensuing explosion lifted it up through the roof and into this level. It stuck out of the floor like a sore mouth, black and cracked, finally out of commission but ever present.

One of Peterkin's forces used it as a kind of ladder as she clambered toward the stairway and Quidler's bunch. It was my idea that Peterkin couldn't have tampered with so many packs, that he had no more advantage than Quidler who manipulated his troops with a driver's hat. I sent out a feeler to the woman climbing around the rim of the vat, told her to fall in and was gratified when she acquiesced. It had been a long time since anyone paid any attention to my wishes.

Peterkin had probably always been a dirty fighter and he was one now. Quidler couldn't quite bring himself to committing his side to wholesale violence, but his opponent harbored no such qualms and armed his side with axes, hatchets, knives, clubs and chains. Quidler's group carried pieces of pipe.

The aggressors made a strong try at gaining the stairs but in the end their weapons defeated them. An axe had to be wielded with two hands, a hatchet stroke was necessarily short, a swing with a knife wasn't always certain, while it was relatively easy to aim a pipe at a head.

The woman whom I had directed into the cold vat climbed out at Peterkin's urging but heeded me and threw herself at the feet of one of her comrades who in turn tumbled into a swinging length of pipe and lost his pack. Scratch one enemy.

Quidler didn't fight but stood at the top of the stairs and tried not to lose his cool as the workers tore one another to pieces. It was a strangely silent battle punctuated by heavy breathing and grunts but not a single cry or scream. A man tried climbing the railing alongside the stairs, unseen by Quidler, but I spotted him, waited until he was some thirty feet off the floor before suggesting to him that he do a swan dive onto his head.

I had lost most of my empathy with the workers. The death of Frye cured me of that, maybe because I endowed her with too much humanity and realism and when she died too much of myself died with her. I had always known the workers were dead but now I really knew it with my mind. No matter what they looked like, no matter how they reminded me of people I had known or people I wished I knew, they were only so much activated meat.

Directing a woman to crack the kneecap of an enemy, I told her to pound on the back of his neck with her pipe after he was down. Sometimes a command of mine was superseded by one of Peterkin's, at which time we usually struggled for ascendancy for a moment or two, until I took over. He wouldn't have made a very good general because he was too willing to sacrifice individuals in his press to reach the stairs, not realizing that the only way he could get there was by the effort of individuals.

He stood back near the vat and ordered his forces to their destruction. There was little difference in the physical strength of a male or female worker because both were stimulated by artificial means. Both were also clumsy so that many blows went awry or astray, some missed half the mark while only a few landed squarely. Since a worker bled like a living person, there was a mess on the floor. A painless confrontation, the war waged until Peterkin was left with a pile of destroyed bodies on his side while Quidler still had three good ones.

Limbs lay like abandoned articles, legs, arms, a few heads, creating no less gruesome a scene because the owners had been dead and unfeeling at the start.

"The place is mine!" Peterkin cried, blood-spattered, crazy, an axe in one hand. "I won!"

"You lost!" yelled Quidler. "Throw down that weapon and get up here where I can handcuff you!"

Peterkin wouldn't come, stumbled among his crippled and deactivated soldiers in search of one to stand up for him. One managed to slither toward the stairs but his armless assault didn't even draw Quidler's attention. Another raised his legless self from a pile of corpses, dripping and ugly enough to cause his commander to cry out and swing the axe at his neck.

"I own this place and I want everyone to do what I say!" Peterkin howled. He kicked a corpse, cursed and leaped back when it reached for his foot. "No wonder I do crazy things!" he said. "Nothing is normal or natural on this world!"

He tried to axe the two workers Quidler sent after him but I made them nimble, had them circle him and approach him from different directions. Emotionally overwrought, unstable and yet savage, he tried a slashing movement at the legs of one and at the same time the other gave him a solid fist to the side of the head.

That was how the war ended, with the enemy general out cold on a mound of dead. At least there would be no problem of whether to evacuate the workers or leave them behind. There were half a dozen or so whole ones left.

I wondered where Peterkin's gun was and why he hadn't used it. Now I know he was too cunning. He was a fox. It was his last ace and he knew he had poor aim and might miss Quidler, besides which he would still have me to contend with. Crippled I might be but unless he got me with a bullet in the head or heart I could break him in two. So he kept his gun hidden and didn't use it until it was terribly to his advantage to do so.

Chapter 24

The evacuation continued as though the war had never happened. The fifth level where it took place flooded so that now only the sixth floor remained habitable. There was food stacked in boxes against a far wall, every rope in the compound lay in a high pile in one corner, a stack of clothing took up too much space. The latter hadn't been essential after all when it became apparent that instead of the water causing the air temperature to plunge it was actually raising it.

There were no corridors on the sixth level, only a series of large rooms, the most northern of which was the popular one because it had the widest window through which everyone was trying to escape. A small hurricane blew outside. That, plus the dark sky and thrashing water, were sufficient to ensure that once a flunky guided a boatload to the steeple he didn't return. Still there was no shortage of crafts, Bates having made certain that anything buoyant was snagged and moored near the window.

Three of the agents Sanderson had brought with him and a couple of cooks went along with Quidler in a large boat and cast off toward the black and distant reaches. I was glad Quidler got away, glad he didn't go in our ill-fated boat, not that I liked him any better now than in the beginning. He handled himself well in the crisis and he was a hard worker, I had to admit, even though I couldn't stand his personality. I stood off to myself and watched his little group go bobbing away atop an insane frenzy of wind and water.

What the planet would eventually become I didn't know. It was possible that it would be nothing more than a whirling storm in the void of space, but somehow I thought not. Such an environment didn't suit the gentle makeup of the frogs, and it was my opinion that one day the wind would cease and Land's End would be a calm sea.

Hourly the underground hotsprings that had been covered for millennia were opening up. Once the ice cap over the large volcano melted somewhat, the deep magma expanded, broke through icewalls and formed hot tributaries that traveled to other mountains. Now the entire planet was gobbling its frozen waste and before long everything would be submerged save for a couple of granite tips. I expected that upon one of them would rest the atomic engine that had begun it all. One day in the far future the comet that controlled this world's environment would return to alter conditions again. Hopefully by then the frogs would have polished their unique skills and could interfere.

Whatever happened, it wasn't going to help us now. The water was splashing through the window and onto the floor by the time Bates readied the last boat. Besides herself, there were two of Sanderson's agents and Peterkin.

The agents had a fit because she insisted upon taking me and the three remaining workers along.

A big insulting mouth attached to an overweight mass named Carson opened his facial orifice and sounded off with a string of the bluest language I had ever heard.

"Not with me, you don't, my lady!" he said by way of finishing, his face puffy with emotion. "I've been walking among these stiffs ever since I got here and I'm blast if I see why I have to ride out with them!"

Exhausted to the point of having to lean against the wall to stay on her feet, Bates used the controller in her pocket to summon a worker. He braced himself in the open window, hauled on a towline and brought our boat toward him.

"You don't have to ride with them," she said. "Stay here. Better yet, get your own boat."

The thought of riding through the storm by himself made Carson turn green. "You're responsible for my safety!" he yelled. "The same as you were supposed to look out for Dick!" He was referring to Sanderson.

"Take that up with him." Bates motioned to Peterkin who sat bound and gagged in a corner.

"You were responsible to see that he behaved!"

"How could I do that? Oh, shut up! The workers are coming with us. If you continue to object I'll have one of them pitch you out into the water."

"Why do they have to come?"

"They're valuable property and I happen to like them. They make better company than a lot of live people I know."

Silenced, at least for the time being, Carson sat against a wall shivering and muttering about the many negative reports he intended submitting once he reached Eden.

The worker in the window got the boat moored fast against the sill and held it while people piled in. At the last minute Bates untied Peterkin and followed him aboard. He went meekly enough, choosing a seat at the other end away from me, now and then casting furtive glances my way.

I sat with my back to the railing and watched the roof of the compound recede into the darkness. Not a particle of regret or nostalgia entered my soul as I saw the water rush in the open window through which we had just escaped. My life was always like that, me leaving somewhere and not regretting that I did so. A lot of hard work and the loss of some friends had been my lot on Land's End, coupled with a mountain of bruises. The rocking of the fragile canvas and rubber container beneath and around me reminded me of how sore I was.

We workers sat in the bow while the others rested near Bates who operated the rudder and kept an eye on a device in her free hand. It was a receiver that blinked blue as long as she was on a straight course toward the steeple. I tried to see Peterkin's face but he sat hunched over with his chin on his knees. He hadn't uttered a sound since we left the building. I hoped he was thinking about all his sins but I doubted it.

A weak gray dawn found us in the middle of a heaving ocean. I was seasick along with everyone else but they were free to hang over the side while I was forced to stifle my inclinations. For several hours the steeple had been visible on the horizon as an undistinguishable lump but gradually it took on the shape of a spire.

Sanderson's agents had been urging Bates to hurry, as if she wasn't already coaxing everything possible out of the sled engines. We all knew that the launching pit inside the space structure was bound to flood at anytime, which meant the ship would be elevated to the next higher pit, a mile up. Not only would the lower pit be full of water but before long the entry doors would be submerged, making it impossible for us to get inside the normal way.

"Can't you go any faster?" snapped Carson. For the past twenty minutes he had been standing in the boat with a hand shading his eyes. He couldn't see anymore than the rest of us but I guess it eased some of his anxiety to pretend that he could.

"She's doing the best she can," said one of his companions. "Sit down and conserve your strength."

We might have made it if one of the engines hadn't died. Of course there was always the possibility that some straggler gaining entry into the steeple would have used the emergency elevator built on the outside and neglected to send it back down. By this time the launch pit had to be flooded and everybody had moved to the next highest level. However we weren't worried about that as we drifted with only one small engine to propel us. All we wanted to do was arrive at the steeple and make use of the equipment that had been left at our disposal. Whatever the rescue squads in the launch tower could do to help us, they would have done, and we would find out what it was when we got there.

Carson was all for pitching me and the other workers over the side but Bates refused, saying it wouldn't make the engine that much more efficient. I think it probably would have but she was committed and wouldn't change her mind. The rubber sides around us were too high to make rowing with our hands feasible so we sat watching the light in the sky make the space structure loom on the horizon like a tower of Babel, unreachable and useless. All we could do was wait for the slight current and the effort of one engine to carry us there.

We were by far too late and knew it before we approached anywhere near the first metal bulwarks, not that the personnel inside hadn't done everything they could for us. Without knowing if anyone else was coming, they made certain the elevator was standing by and had even left buoyant platforms for us to stand on while we were boarding.

It was the water that did us in, the constantly rising tide creeping up and ever upward while we wondered if our one engine would hold out. We still couldn't see clearly enough to discover how badly the lower level had flooded, but everyone except Peterkin was optimistic and held out hope that we would be successful.

It didn't seem to be in his plans that we ever reached the steeple because we still had a good way to go when he pulled a rubber wrapping loose from the inside of his boot, took out a gun and ordered us all to jump overboard.

"For Heaven's sake, you can't mean it!" cried Carson, standing up again. He was near enough to the railing that when Peterkin shot him he fell backward and went over into the sea.

I guess he had been waiting until he sighted the large orange buoy floating off the port bow before he risked confronting us. Before his last return to the compound he must have taken a loose boat, secured it to a line and a float and left it there close to the steeple for later use. Why hadn't he joined the first refugee groups and been rescued earlier? For one thing, he had to come back and take care of Bates. For another, he intended to get away scot free altogether, figured that if he waited until the last minute there wouldn't be anyone left in the launcher who knew him by sight. He planned to show up late with a phony name, travel to Eden and eventually to Earth as someone else. What he had in mind to do once he finally arrived home remained his secret.

I reasoned this out later but at the moment I was waiting for him to turn his gun on me and blast out my lights. Instead he paid no attention to me, no doubt more concerned with the bright people in the group than the dim ones.

Actually he had already made his choice as to which of us he hated the most. It was Bates who won by a wide margin.

Peterkin had no wish to shoot us all. He hadn't enough bullets and he was getting nervous because there didn't appear to be any overt activity around the steeple. It was yet in the distance and the boat rocked so that we couldn't get a clear view, but we ought to at least have been able to see the elevator going up and down.

He was curiously calm in his actions, which was probably the result of a volume of swallowed tranquilizers. Still, he was cold-blooded enough as he pointed the gun at the bottom of the boat and fired three shots.

Immediately we began to founder. The taut rubber hull

sagged and took in water while everyone started screaming. Except for Bates. She seemed to have it in mind to
grapple with Peterkin and hurled herself at him and it was
at that moment that I think he finally made up his mind
between the two of us. Raising the gun, he hit her hard
on the side of the head, a deliberate blow calculated to
knock her out so that when she fell over the side she
would quickly drown.

The last thing I saw as the boat sank under me was
Peterkin swimming away toward the orange buoy.
Meanwhile I headed to the bottom in a hurry, weighted
down by my clothes and the shoulder cast. Maybe I could
have made it if I had been in good shape. I don't know.
I'll never know and I'll never forget that day.

Not a good swimmer to begin with, I battled gravity,
even yanked on the sodden cast until it came loose from
my shoulder. It wasn't enough. No matter how I tried to
swim to the spot where Bates had gone down, I made
poor headway. In a little while I made no movements forward at all but merely sank.

I did my drowning all by myself with no idea of where
anyone else was. They couldn't have had much of a
chance, what with their terror and the wind-whipped sea
building waves twenty feet high. I kept going deeper and
all the time I was thinking of the first time I had
drowned. Now I remembered how the boat had capsized
and how I sank among the green reeds at the bottom of
the lake. There were no reeds or anything here except
dark water and a terrible shortage of air.

At first it was frightening, mostly because I knew the
others were dying while I could do nothing to help them,
but then it became quiet and peaceful around me. I
couldn't see or hear but I could feel the ice beneath my
fingertips. My shoulder no longer hurt, my throat didn't
feel clogged anymore, my heart beat began to fade like a
drum that grew softer and softer until it was finally
silenced.

My first thought when I opened my eyes was that the
frogs had let me down. Somewhere in my hazy mind was

the memory of Felix promising to keep an eye out for rescue boats. It was foolish of me to believe they were omnipotent creatures when they actually and plainly led hit-and-miss existences. It wouldn't be easy for them to relearn how to be more aquatic than dry-land people and in fact the time would come when they built floating cities and lived in them most of the time, but for now they had an endless ocean with which to become familiar and couldn't be blamed if they missed a boat or two of refugees. That they deeply regretted having missed mine I could tell by the way Felix knelt beside my body and wept.

It was very strange watching him do that. Like an observer in a dream I lay on a raft and watched my little gray friend grieve over my unattractive remains. Now more than ever I could see how homely I was, flopped on the raft like a beached whale with my hair plastered across my face and my dead eyes staring up at the sky.

It jolted me to look at my eyes and realize that I was deader than I would ever be again. This time no doctors were going to open my head and make me walk again, no, not by a long shot, because all I was truly fit for now was fishfood. Felix touched my crushed shoulder and blubbered anew, brushed my hair off my forehead and broke out into more sobbing, and all the time I lay wondering what kind of crazy nightmare I was having.

"Don't do that, I'm not worth it," I said, or tried to say, in the old mind language I had always used with him. There was something different about my head. Besides hurting like the devil, it was missing something that made it possible for me to talk to Felix. He didn't turn toward me, never even heard me but continued crying and caressing my corpse.

My eyes smarting, I stared about and saw that we were alone on the raft, just me and my gray friend. He must have confiscated it from the sea, located my carcass and hauled it out of the water, and now he was holding some kind of funeral service.

"Felix, you idiot, quit that!" I croaked. "I wouldn't

have wanted you to bawl over me while I was alive and now that I'm dead will you kindly shut up and just tip me over the side?"

To my horror that's exactly what he did, leaned his weight against my side, elevated a thigh and shoved until I slowly went over. I hadn't really meant it and tried to tell him so but my head wasn't working right and I was unable to communicate with him. I wanted to tell him to hang onto that body because there was still some life in it. After all, here I was thinking up a storm, feeling light in my eyes, experiencing an intense pain in the side of my head. Didn't that mean I wasn't dead, and there the fool frog had dumped me into the drink?

Limp as a string, unable to cry out, I watched my remains float for a second or two before sinking into the briny. Believing I was having an out-of-the body experience, I expected to suddenly find myself sinking like a stone again, but it didn't happen. I still lay on the rubber with a sore head, blinking my eyes as I watched myself disappear from sight. For a moment self-pity slammed at me and I almost wept, too, but then I remembered that I had spent twenty-four miserable years in that large bag of bones, so good riddance, let me sink forever from sight and never be heard from again.

I surprised myself by hiccupping, which made no sense at all if I was dead in the water. I raised my head and looked at Felix who was waving goodbye to his friend. "Hey, it's okay, something funny is going on and I'm not really dead, I'm over here!" I wanted to say to him, and I tried, but he only understood mind language and couldn't hear me.

It began to get to me and I tried bellowing. If there was anything I hated it was a mystery. By rights I ought to be so much expired meat and not lying here staring at my own hand. Except that it wasn't my hand, which made the mystery deeper, because it was certainly mine since it was attached to me and full of feeling. Yet never had I possessed such small fingers and delicate painted nails. I was built like a truck and right then and there I liked my big body and wanted it back.

"No!" I said to Felix. He was there in front of me now, standing over me, and he wasn't crying anymore but was smiling. All at once he knelt, picked up the hand that bewildered me so and kissed it. I knew it must have hurt him to come into contact with me that way but he didn't seem to mind, covered it with affection and even planted a kiss on my cheek.

"I can't have a cheek!" I croaked. It was a real voice but not one I recognized as me. "My cheek just sank in the ocean," I said. "I saw it. So did my hands, my legs, my head. . . ."

I was still in possession of all those items and the knowledge upset me horribly. Big tears spilled from my eyes and I made snuffling noises. Felix patted me and then indicated that I had no more time to feel sorry for myself but must get up and get the devil out of there. How could I? My brain was whirling so rapidly that I didn't know which way was up. Again I raised a hand and looked at it. Strange but mine. The same thing could be said for the legs, the torso and the rest. The only trouble was that I had never seen them on me before in my life. Then all at once I stared long and hard at the jeans I was wearing, especially at the little brass buttons along the beltline. I had seen those buttons and jeans a dozen times but they had been on the body of Shirley Bates.

Slowly I looked from the buttons to Felix' face and realized that he was staring back at me with a mixture of sadness and happiness. My little friend to the end, he had done what he could for me, whether I approved of it or not. This was no out-of-the-body experience for me but a real, three-dimensional one. My body was at the bottom of the sea while I lay here on a rubber float breathing in good air and watching my frog friend who was trying to tell me I hadn't much time.

I knew what he meant. The steeple was close enough for me to see that not only had the water risen up over the launching pit but it reached halfway up to the third level, which meant that if I wanted to live I had to climb a sheer mile of girders.

"I'm no thief that I have to steal her body!" I said aloud. At the exact same instant, the hair on the back of my neck stirred because a faint little voice in my head said, "It's all yours, kid, and you're welcome."

I'll always believe it was Bates, there one moment in the body, or at least a part of her lingered long enough to tell me it was all right and that she understood. Then the small bit of her was gone, as if she had never inhabited this shell, leaving me as the sole tenant. But I knew what I had heard and it made me feel a little better. This body was my house whether I wanted it or not and there was no one else around to claim it.

Standing up, I realized how well I felt. And, good grief, I was intelligent! Oh, I don't mean unlearned facts flowed through my head, but the knowledge I had was there at my disposal so that I wouldn't have to stammer and stutter as I went searching through my memories for answers and meanings, as I had in the past.

Desiring that I survive in any shape or form, Felix took my hand and pointed at the steeple. He had done what he could for me, salvaged my dying body and used kanalba to transfer my spirit into Bates' newly dead corpse. Now the rest was up to me. Could I climb up the steeple to the nearest entrance before the last ship left this planet?

How was it to be possible for me to even walk in this small frame after having inhabited a huge and powerful one? Stretching my legs and arms, I looked up at the spires. The raft rocked and bucked under my feet but I had no trouble maintaining my balance. It was because my brain was normal. No more clumsiness, no more gross bulk, no more tripping and stumbling, no more weird complexes. More significant than that, no more ugliness and stupidity.

Those last thoughts were enough to instill in me a sense of haste. I could survive if I remained here on this watery globe, so that meant I had to climb the steeple. Turning to Felix, I threw my arms around him and hugged him tight. Then I picked up the oar lying at my feet and paddled toward the nearest metal struts.

I took hold of one and began climbing a series of bars shaped almost like a ladder. I soon began to believe there was no way I could make it, but I didn't want Felix to know it. He stayed on the raft until I was a mere dot in the sky before diving into his world and disappearing. When I saw him do that, I stopped where I was and assessed my situation. This would be a good spot from which to do a swan dive. I would never live through the fall, my troubles would be over and that would be the end of it.

Unfortunately or no, I wasn't made that way, besides which I no longer inhabited a defective, good-for-nothing body but a perfectly healthy one that was scarcely out of breath after a long and arduous climb. Bates had weighed about one hundred and twenty pounds, not small but certainly not large, not particularly muscular but not soft either. Her job had kept her in strong physical condition so that as I clung to the girders and looked out over my glittering environment the idea came to me that I had a chance of pulling it off. Down there on the raft I hadn't really believed it but up here where I could breathe I wasn't so pessimistic. The metal was damp and now and then I would have to stop and rest, but there was really nothing between me and safety except a bit of distance.

No, there was something else between me and the next operating level of the steeple and that was the person climbing the struts a quarter-mile ahead of me. He was the real reason why I decided to try saving myself instead of diving off the height. I knew who he was and the knowledge fortified my intent to continue climbing, to catch up with him and to throw him out into space.

My one regret in losing the body that had always been a burden to me was that much strength had been lost with it. Forever after today, I would be at a physical disadvantage with half the world's adult population, though thinking about it and accepting the fact didn't overly disturb me. Nearly all women had been at such a disadvantage, for always, yet they seemed to be coping well enough. I vowed that I would, too. I would take Bates' body and use it to pursue a decent future, just as soon as I gave her murderer what was coming to him.

I don't know when he realized someone else was climbing after him. It made sense that at least one more straggler would have survived the water, and he or she could have come from any of the compounds. Not that Peterkin intended taking any chances. As soon as he reached the catwalk below the third entrance into the space launcher, he crouched down and waited until I came into view.

I knew he wouldn't be expecting Bates to come puffing and grunting up those struts, not after the way he had clobbered her with his gun. Funny how I readily accepted Shirley Bates as my outer form that day, and it was almost cheerfully that I shoved off from one metal bar only to grasp another and haul on it. One or two people were destined to take a long fall within the next hour or so, but either way or whichever number it turned out to be, Peterkin was going to get very wet.

The sun was mostly hidden by cloud banks but a few rays sneaked through to glance off the steeple and make it a glistening shard. I could see Peterkin clearly now and I stayed in plain sight because I wanted to see his face when he recognized me.

He was like a spider sneaking behind bars and struts as he cast glances down at me, scurrying along the catwalk, first making certain his next step would be a safe one before looking back down at me. Even before he knew who it was in pursuit, he wasted his last two bullets firing at me. They came nowhere near me and neither did the gun which he hurled in my direction. Fool that he was, he hadn't taken the time to discover if I was a friend or foe. Or maybe he knew. Maybe his conscience had caught up with him, tricking him into thinking the shadow on his trail was an avenging angel.

Not feeling anything like an angel, I hauled myself on up the ladder, climbed over the catwalk railing and ran in the same direction he had taken. Aware that he might be waiting for me around the next bend, I took to some higher struts and labored until I came upon him crouching and waiting. As he looked up and saw me, his eyes widened, his face went pale with shock. Maybe there was something odd about my expression but he didn't react as if he were being pursued by a woman much smaller than himself. Leaping erect, he ran on around the walk and disappeared from sight.

Sooner or later it would have to occur to him that the people inside the steeple would become aware of our presence. There were thick panes of glass everywhere on the walls in this section and every so often I caught a glimmer of movement beyond them. Very soon someone was bound to open the door and come out to investigate.

I underestimated Peterkin's madness but not his intelligence. Just about the time I began getting uneasy because I hadn't seen him for a while, I looked up and spotted him clambering down the struts toward me. He had climbed above me while he was out of sight, done exactly what I would have done in his place, not that it would do me any good to realize he was a step ahead of me. No one with any sense would do what he was about to do, but then good sense had never been one of his strong points.

Before I could get off the struts and back down onto the walk again, he let go with his toes, dangled several feet above me, hung on with his hands and kicked me off my perch. I was so surprised that I fell several yards, banging my hands on the bars, before I made a serious effort to grab one and stop my flight. It wasn't easy adjusting to such a small body, though lightness was an advantage. No one would have been able to kick my other body loose like that, but I needed to remember that I didn't have it anymore, that it was at the bottom of this world. Now I had a slight but tough body and I had best not forget it.

Clearly disappointed because I hadn't dropped to my death, Peterkin clambered down toward me, full of confidence, almost eager as he moved from strut to strut. He might not have been so avid had he been aware that I didn't know what it was to be afraid. Not of something like this. Oh, people could scare the daylights out of me but only if they smiled at me, asked me questions or wanted to use me as a guinea pig. I might be Bates on the outside but inside I was still me.

Quickly I climbed out of Peterkin's way and faced him on a straight level, face to face, close enough to see the sweat beads on his forehead. It was warm on the steeple so he had discarded everything but his pants. I kept my longsleeved shirt because it afforded me some friction whenever I leaned against the metal. Now I leaned back because I knew he was going to jump me, and jump he did, like a wild man, straight at me with his fingers curved like claws. I guess Bates had been one of his special hates for a long time.

His fingers closed on nothing but struts because I wasn't there anymore. Instead of moving away by clinging to the holds face-first, I rolled from back to front in even movements, grasping and swinging my way along while Peterkin came after me. He made little screeching sounds like an agitated monkey, kicked at the metal with his feet, reached hungrily for me, too out of breath to curse.

Facing the steeple, getting a good grip with my feet on some lower bars, I stayed where I was and watched his face. Smiling because he thought I was exhausted, he braced himself with his feet and his left hand, held his other fist up and out, leaned toward me and took a swing. In a flash I ducked so that he slammed against the bar over my head. While he bellowed and came after me, I scooted between two struts, turned my back, pushed myself hard against the wall so that I was a little hard ball.

He couldn't see me because I was so small, and that was what I had in mind. Weak Shirley Bates crouched in the niche between struts but big old ugly me waited for Peterkin to appear before me.

He did, ferocious and triumphant, sure that he had me trapped in a corner like a desperate rabbit. I have no doubt that it went my way because I wasn't afraid of him and still had memories of living in a powerful body.

His arms and legs wide, he planted himself firmly in front of me, grinned and reached for me. That was when I struck, in the instant that he dropped one hand free from a hold. Then my feet, with all my strength behind them, and perhaps some of my lost strength, hit him squarely in the chest.

He hadn't been expecting it. Why should he? After all, I was the underdog, full of fear and misgivings because I was outmatched all the way. Too bad. It was his error. His last one, I might add. He hadn't that good a grip with his one hand, most of his weight being forward toward me while his toes maintained most of his balance. An expression of incredulity wiped the glee from his face just before he flew backward and went tumbling head over heels into the grayness of space.

Dizzy and feeling sick, I stayed where I was and panted through my open mouth. Down and down Peterkin fell in silence, slowly and without grace, until the mist took command to hide him from me.

A few minutes later I stood on the catwalk pounding on the steeple door. A man I had never seen before opened it, stared at me with a startled but pleased expression and said, "You just cost me fifty bucks!"

This was the moment I was really afraid of, the moment when somebody normal looked at me as another normal person and spoke to me. I could either speak back or retreat into my complex.

"What do you mean?" I croaked.

"My buddy bet me that some poor desperate maniac would climb the outside of this monster and I said no way!"

I smiled and made as if to walk past him.

"Hey, you look like you've been through a war!" He lent me a hand and I was glad to take it.

"That isn't all that's wrong with me," I said. "I was bumped on the head and can't remember a thing."

Attention:

DAW COLLECTORS

Many readers of DAW Books have written requesting information on early titles and book numbers to assist in the collection of DAW editions since the first of our titles appeared in April 1972.

We have prepared a several-pages-long list of all DAW titles, giving their sequence numbers, original and current order numbers, and ISBN numbers. And of course the authors and book titles, as well as reissues.

If you think that this list will be of help, you may have a copy by writing to the address below and enclosing one dollar in stamps or coins to cover the handling and postage costs.

DAW BOOKS, INC. Dept. C
1633 Broadway
New York, N.Y. 10019

DAW presents TANITH LEE

"A brilliant supernova in the firmament of SF"—**Progressef**